it again. Then he watched it a third time. There had to be something he was missing, because he couldn't pick out a single giveaway.

"If she's cheating," Al said with something like respect, "she's the best I've ever seen."

"What does your gut say?" Dante trusted his chief of security. Al had spent thirty years in the casino business, and some people swore he could spot cheats as soon as they walked in the door. If Al thought she was cheating, then Dante would take action—and he wouldn't be watching this tape now if something hadn't made Al uneasy.

Al scratched the side of his jaw, considering. He was a big, bulky man, but no one who observed him for any length of time would think he was slow, either physically or mentally. Finally he said, "If she isn't cheating, she's the luckiest person walking. She wins. Week in, week out, she wins. Never a huge amount, but I ran the numbers, and she's into us for about five grand a week. Hell, boss, on her way out of the casino she'll stop by a slot machine, feed a dollar in and walk away with at least fifty. It's never the same machine, either. I've had her watched, I've had her followed, I've even looked for the same faces in the casino every time she's in here, and I can't find a common denominator."

"Is she here now?"

"She came in about half an hour ago. She's playing blackjack, as usual."

"Who's the dealer?"

"Cindy."

Cindy Josephson was Dante's best dealer, almost as sharp at spotting a cheater as Al himself. She had been with him since he'd opened Inferno, and he trusted her to run an honest game. "Bring the woman to my office," Dante said, making a swift decision. "Don't make a scene."

"Got it," said Al, turning on his heel and leaving the security center, where banks of monitors displayed every angle of the casino.

Dante left, too, going up to his office. His face was calm. Normally he would leave it to Al to deal with a cheater, but he was curious. How was she doing it? There were a lot of bad cheaters, a few good ones, and every so often one would come along who was the stuff of which legends were made: the cheater who didn't get caught, even when people were alert and the camera was on him—or, in this case, her.

It was possible for people to simply be lucky, as most people understood luck. Chance could turn a habitual loser into a big-time winner. Casinos, in fact, thrived on that hope. But luck itself wasn't habitual, and he knew that what passed for luck was often something else: cheating. Then there

LINDA HOWARD

Linda Howard says that whether she's reading them or writing them, books have long played a profound role in her life. She cut her teeth on Margaret Mitchell and from then on continued to read widely and eagerly. In recent years her interest has settled on romance fiction, because she's "easily bored by murder, mayhem and politics." After twenty-one years of penning stories for her own enjoyment, Ms. Howard finally worked up the courage to submit a novel for publication—and met with success. This Alabama native is now a multi–*New York Times* bestselling author.

LINDA HOWARD

RAINTREE:
Inferno

Silhouette Books

nocturne™

SILHOUETTE BOOKS

ISBN-13: 978-0-373-61762-3
ISBN-10:   0-373-61762-3

RAINTREE: INFERNO

Dear Reader,

My friends Beverly, Linda and I have worked on the concept for these books for about four years, spent hours and hours discussing them, playing with ideas and laughing our heads off. Not that these books are funny, but after a while we got sort of punch-drunk and we'd go off on tangents. One such tangent was limericks (*There was a young man from Paducah...*), which of course had nothing to do with the Raintree books.

We loved working out the mythology behind the Raintree, extraordinary people trying to live in the ordinary world without being found out. We loved the characters. They are all very human, and at the same time they are...more than human. I hope you enjoy them, too.

Linda

To Beverly Barton and Linda Winstead Jones,
for the years of friendship and all the fun we had
planning these books, and to Leslie Wainger, for
being everything an editor should be,
as well as a friend.

Chapter 1

Sunday

Dante Raintree stood with his arms crossed as he watched the woman on the monitor. The image was in black and white, to better show details; color distracted the brain. He focused on her hands, watching every move she made, but what struck him most was how uncommonly *still* she was. She didn't fidget, or play with her chips, or look around at the other players. She peeked once at her down card, then didn't touch it again, signaling for another hit by tapping a fingernail on the table. Just because she didn't seem to be paying attention to the other players, though, didn't mean she was as unaware as she seemed.

"What's her name?" he asked.

"Lorna Clay," replied his chief of security, Al Rayburn.

"Is that her real name?"

"It checks out."

If Al hadn't already investigated her, Dante would have been disappointed. He paid Al a lot of money to be efficient and thorough.

"At first I thought she was counting," said Al. "But she doesn't pay enough attention."

"She's paying attention, all right," Dante murmured. "You just don't see her doing it." A card counter had to remember every card played. Supposedly counting cards was impossible with the number of decks used by the casinos, but no casino wanted a card counter at its tables. There *were* those rare individuals who could calculate the odds even with multiple decks.

"I thought that, too," said Al. "But look at this piece of tape coming up. Someone she knows comes up to her and speaks, she looks around and starts chatting, completely misses the play of the people to her left—and doesn't look around even when the deal comes back to her, she just taps that finger. And damned if she didn't win. Again."

Dante watched the tape, rewound it, watched

was the other kind of luck, the kind he himself possessed, but since it depended not on chance but on who and what he was, he knew it was an innate power and not Dame Fortune's erratic smiles. Since his power was rare, the odds made it likely the woman he'd been watching was merely a very clever cheat.

Her skill could provide her with a very good living, he thought, doing some swift calculations in his head. Five grand a week equaled two hundred sixty thousand dollars a year, and that was just from his casino. She probably hit all of them, careful to keep the numbers relatively low so she stayed under the radar.

He wondered how long she'd been taking him, how long she'd been winning a little here, a little there, before Al noticed.

The curtains were still open on the wall-to-wall window in his office, giving the impression, when one first opened the door, of stepping out onto a covered balcony. The glazed window faced west, so he could catch the sunsets. The sun was low now, the sky painted in purple and gold. At his home in the mountains, most of the windows faced east, affording him views of the sunrise. Something in him needed both the greeting and the goodbye of the sun. He'd always been drawn to sunlight, maybe because fire was his element to call, to control.

He checked his internal time: four minutes until sundown. He knew exactly, without checking the tables every day, when the sun would slide behind the mountains. He didn't own an alarm clock. He didn't need one. He was so acutely attuned to the sun's position that he had only to check within himself to know the time. As for waking at a particular time, he was one of those people who could tell himself to wake at a certain time, and he did. That particular talent had nothing to do with being Raintree, so he didn't have to hide it; a lot of perfectly ordinary people had the same ability.

There were other talents and abilities, however, that did require careful shielding. The long days of summer instilled in him an almost sexual high, when he could feel contained power buzzing just beneath his skin. He had to be doubly careful not to cause candles to leap into flame just by his presence, or to start wildfires, with a glance, in the dry-as-tinder brush. He loved Reno; he didn't want to burn it down. He just felt so damn *alive* with all the sunshine pouring down that he wanted to let the energy pour through him instead of holding it inside.

This must be how his brother Gideon felt while pulling lightning, all that hot power searing through his muscles, his veins. They had this in common, the connection with raw power. All the members of the far-flung Raintree clan had some power, some heightened form of ability, but only members of the royal family could channel and control the earth's natural energies.

Dante wasn't just of the royal family; he was the Dranir, the leader of the entire clan. "Dranir" was synonymous with "king," but the position he held wasn't ceremonial, it was one of sheer power. He was the oldest son of the previous Dranir, but he would have been passed over for the position if he hadn't also inherited the power to hold it.

Gideon was second to him in power; if anything happened to Dante and he died without a child who had inherited his abilities, Gideon would become Dranir—a possibility that filled his brother with dread, hence the fertility charm currently lying on Dante's desk. It had arrived in the mail just that morning. Gideon regularly sent them, partly as a joke, but mainly because he was doing all he could to insure that Dante had offspring— thus upping the chances that *he* would never inherit the position. Whenever they managed to get together, Dante had to carefully search every nook and cranny, as well as all his clothing, to make certain Gideon hadn't left one of his clever little charms in a hidden place.

Gideon was getting better at making them, Dante mused. Practice made perfect, after all, and God knows he'd made plenty of the charms in the past few years. Not only were they more potent now, but he varied his approach. Some of them were obvious, silver pieces meant to be worn around the neck like an amulet—not that Dante was an amulet kind of guy. Others were tiny, subtle, like the one Gideon had embedded in the newest business card he'd sent, knowing Dante would likely tuck the card into his pocket. He'd erred only in that the very power of the charm gave it away; Dante had sensed the buzz of its power, though he'd had the devil's own time finding it.

Behind him came Al's distinctive *knock-knock* on the door. The outer office was empty, Dante's secretary having gone home hours before. "Come in," he called, not turning from his view of the sunset.

The door opened, and Al said, "Mr. Raintree, this is Lorna Clay."

Dante turned and looked at the woman, all his senses on alert. The first thing he noticed was the vibrant color of her hair—a rich, dark red that encompassed a multitude of shades from copper to burgundy. The warm amber light danced along the iridescent strands, and he felt a hard tug of sheer lust in his gut. Looking at her hair was almost like looking at fire, and he had the same reaction.

The second thing he noticed was that she was spitting mad.

Chapter 2

Several things happened so closely together that they might as well have been simultaneous. With his senses already so heightened, the quick lash of desire collided with Dante's visceral reaction to fire, sending explosions of sensation cascading along all his neural pathways, too fast for him to control. Across the room, he saw all the candles leap with fire, the wicks burning too fast, too wild, so that the multiple little flames flared larger and more brightly than they should. And on his desk, Gideon's damn little fertility charm began to buzz with power, as if it had an on/off switch that had suddenly been pressed.

What the hell…?

He didn't have time to dissect and analyze everything that was going on; he had to control himself, and fast, or the entire room would be ablaze. He hadn't suffered such a humiliating loss of control of his powers since he'd first entered puberty and his surging hormones had played hell with everything.

Ruthlessly, he began exerting his will on all that leaping power. It wasn't easy; though he held himself perfectly still, mentally he felt as if he were riding a big, nasty-tempered bull. The natural inclination of energy was to be free, and it resisted any effort to tame it, to wrestle it back inside his mental walls. His control was usually phenomenal. After all, *having* power wasn't what made a Dranir; having it and *controlling* it *was*. Lack of control led to devastation—and ultimately to exposure. The Raintree had survived the centuries due in large part to their ability to blend with normal people, so it wasn't a matter to be taken lightly.

Dante had trained all his life to master the power and energies that ran through him, and even though he knew that as the summer solstice drew near his control was always stretched a bit, he wasn't accustomed to this degree of difficulty. Grimly he concentrated, pulling back, clamping down, exerting his will over the very forces of nature. He could have extinguished the candles, but with an even greater force of will he left them burning, for to make the tiny flames wink out now might draw even more attention than lighting them in the first place.

The only thing that evaded his control was that damn fertility charm on his desk, buzzing and throbbing and all but sending out a strobe effect. Even though he knew Al and Ms. Clay couldn't pick up on the energy the thing was sending out, not glancing at it took all his self-control. Gideon had outdone himself with this one. Just wait until the next time he saw his little brother, Dante grimly promised himself. If Gideon thought this was funny, they would both see how funny it was when the tables were turned. Gideon wasn't the only one who could make fertility charms.

All the wildfires once more under control, he returned his attention to his guest.

Lorna once again tried to twist her arm away from the gorilla holding her, but his grip was just strong enough to hold without applying undue pressure. While a small part of her appreciated that he was actively trying not to hurt her, by far the largest part of her was so furious—and, yes, scared—that she wanted to lash out at him with all her strength, clawing and kicking and biting, doing anything she could to get free.

Then her survival instinct kicked into high gear and her hair all but stood on end as she realized the man standing so silent and still in front of the huge windows was a far greater threat to her than was the gorilla.

Her throat closed, a fist of fear tightening around her neck. She couldn't have said what it was about him that so alarmed her, but she had felt this way only once before, in a back alley in Chicago. She was accustomed to taking care of herself on the streets and had normally used the alley as a shortcut to her place—a shabby single room in a run-down building—but one night when she had started down the alley, alarm had prickled her scalp and she'd frozen, unable to take another step. She couldn't see anything suspicious, couldn't hear anything, but she could *not* move forward. Her heart had been hammering so hard in her chest she could barely breathe, and she had abruptly been sick with fear. Slowly she had backed out of the alley's entrance and fled down the street to take the long way home.

The next morning a prostitute's body had been found in the alley, brutally raped and mutilated. Lorna knew the dead woman could have been her, if not for the sudden hair-raising panic that had warned her away.

This was the same, like being body-slammed by a sense of danger. The man in front of her, whoever he was, was a threat to her. She doubted—at least on a rational level—that he would murder and mutilate her, but there were other dangers, other destructions she could suffer.

She felt as if she were smothering, her throat so tight very little air could get past the constriction. Pinpricks of light flared at the edges of her vision, and in silent horror she realized she might faint. She didn't dare lose consciousness; she would be completely helpless if she did.

"Miss Clay," he said in a calm, smooth-as-cream voice, as if her panic were completely invisible to him and no one else in the room knew she was on the verge of screaming. "Sit down, please."

The prosaic invitation/command had the blessed effect of snapping her out of the trap of panic. Somehow she managed to take a breath without audibly gasping, then another. Nothing was going to happen. She didn't need to panic. Yes, this was mildly alarming and she probably wouldn't be coming back to the Inferno to gamble, but she hadn't broken any laws or casino rules. She was safe.

Those pinpricks of light flared again. What…? Puzzled, she turned her head and found herself staring at two huge pillar candles, each of them easily two and a half feet tall, one on the floor and the other perched on a slab of white marble that served as a hearth. Flames danced around the candles' multiple wicks.

Candles. She hadn't been about to faint. The flickers of light at the edge of her vision had come from those candles. She hadn't noticed them when she'd been literally dragged into the room, but that was understandable.

The candlelights were dancing and swaying, as if they stood in a draft. That too was understandable. She didn't feel any noticeable movement of air, but this was summertime in Reno, and the air-conditioning would be running full blast. She always wore long sleeves when she went to a casino anyway; otherwise she was too cold.

With a start she realized she was staring at the candles and had neither moved nor replied to the invitation to sit. She jerked her attention back to the man standing at the window, trying to recall what the gorilla had called him. "Who are you?" she demanded sharply. Once more she jerked her arm, but the gorilla merely sighed as he held her. "Let go!"

"You can let her go," the man said, sounding faintly amused. "Thank you for bringing her here."

The gorilla instantly released her, said, "I'll be in the security center," and quietly let himself out of the office.

Instantly Lorna began assessing her chance of

making a run for it, but for now she stood her ground. She didn't want to run; the casino had her name, her description. If she ran, she would be blacklisted—not just in the Inferno, but in every casino in Nevada.

"I'm Dante Raintree," the man said, then waited a beat to see if she gave any reaction to the name. It meant nothing to her, so she merely gave a slight, questioning lift of her brows. "I own the Inferno."

Crap! An owner carried serious weight with the gaming commission. She would have to tread very carefully, but she had the advantage. He couldn't prove she'd been cheating, because the simple fact was, she hadn't been.

"Dante. Inferno. I get it," she replied with a little edge of *so what?* in her tone. He was probably so rich he thought everyone should be awed in his presence. If he wanted to awe her, he would have to find something other than his wealth to do the job. She appreciated money as much as anyone; it certainly made life easier. Now that she had a little financial cushion, she was amazed at how much better she slept—what a relief it was not to worry where her next bite was coming from, or when. At the same time, she despised people who thought their wealth entitled them to special treatment.

Not only that, his name was ridiculous. Maybe his last name really was Raintree, but he'd probably

chosen his first name for the drama and to fit the
name of the casino. His real first name was
probably something like Melvin or Fred.

"Please have a seat," he invited again, indicating the cream-colored leather sofa to her right. A
jade coffee table sat between the sofa and two
cushy-looking club chairs. She tried not to stare at
the table as she took a seat in one of the chairs,
which was just as cushy as it looked. Surely the
table was just the color of jade and not actually
made of the real stone, but it *looked* real, as if it
were faintly translucent. Surely it was just glass. If
so, the craftsmanship was superb.

Lorna didn't have a lot of experience with
luxury items, but she did have a sort of sixth sense
about her surroundings. She began to feel overwhelmed by the things around her. No, not overwhelmed; that wasn't the right word. She tried to
nail down what she was feeling, but there was an
alien, unknown quality to the very air around her
that she couldn't describe. This was unfamiliar,
and it definitely carried the edge of danger that had
so alarmed her when she'd first become aware of it.

As Dante Raintree strolled closer, she realized
that everything she was sensing centered on him.
She'd been right; *he* was the danger.

He moved with indolent grace, but there was
nothing slow or lazy about him. He was a tall man,

about eight or nine inches taller than her own five foot five, and though his excellently tailored clothing gave him a lean look, there was no tailor skilled enough to completely disguise the power of the muscles beneath the fabric. Not a cheetah, then, but a tiger.

She realized she had avoided looking him full in the face, as if not having that knowledge would give her a small measure of safety. She knew better; ignorance was never a good defense, and Lorna had learned a long time ago not to hide her head in the sand and hope for the best.

He sat down across from her, and with an inward bracing she met his gaze full-on.

The bottom dropped out of her stomach.

She had a faint, dizzying sensation of falling; she barely restrained herself from gripping the arms of the chair to steady herself.

His hair was black. His eyes were green. Common colors, and yet nothing about him was common. His hair was sleek and glossy, falling to his shoulders. She didn't like long hair on men, but his looked clean and soft, and she wanted to bury her hands in it. She shoved *that* idea away and promptly became snagged by his gaze. His eyes weren't just green, they were *green*, so remarkably green that her first thought was that he was wearing colored contacts. A color that darkly rich

and pure couldn't be real. They were just very
realistic contacts, with tiny black striations in
them like real eyes. She had seen ads for those in
magazines. The only thing was, when the candles
flared and his pupils briefly contracted, the color
of his irises seemed to expand. Could contacts
give that appearance?

He wasn't wearing contacts. Instinctively she
knew that everything she saw, from the sleek black-
ness of his hair to that intense eye color, was real.

He was drawing her in. Some power she
couldn't understand was tugging at her with an almost physical sensation. The candle flames were
dancing wildly, brighter now that the sun had set
and twilight was deepening outside the window.
The candles were the only light in the now gloomy
office, sending shadows slashing across the hard
angles of his face, and yet his eyes seemed to glow
brighter with color than they had only a few
moments before.

They hadn't said a word since he'd sat down, yet
she felt as if she were in a battle for her will, her
force, her independent life. Deep inside, panic
flared to candlelight life, dancing and leaping. *He
knows*, she thought, and tensed herself to run.
Forget the casinos, forget the very nice money
she'd been reaping, forget everything except survival. *Run!*

Her body didn't obey. She continued to sit there, frozen...mesmerized.

"How are you doing it?" he finally asked, his tone still as calm and unruffled as if he were oblivious to the swirls and surges of power that were buffeting her.

Once again, his voice seemed to break through her inner turmoil and bring her back to reality. Bewildered, she stared at him. He thought *she* was doing all this weird stuff?

"I'm not," she blurted. "I thought you were."

She might have been mistaken, because in the dancing candlelight, reading an expression was tricky, but she thought he looked slightly stunned.

"Cheating," he said in clarification. "How are you stealing from me?"

Chapter 3

Maybe he didn't know.

His bluntness was a perverse relief. Lorna took a deep breath. At least now she was dealing with something she understood. Ignoring the strange undercurrents in the room, the almost physical sensation of being surrounded by…something…she lifted her chin, narrowed her eyes and gave him stare for stare. "I'm not cheating!" That was true— as far as it went, and in the normal understanding of the word.

"Of course you are. No one is as lucky as you seem to be unless he—excuse me, *she*—is cheating." His eyes were glittering now, but in her book glittering was way better than that weird glowing. Eyes didn't glow anyway. What was wrong with her? Had someone slipped a drug into her drink while her head was turned? She never drank alcohol while she was gambling, sticking to coffee or soft drinks, but that last cup of coffee had tasted bitter. At the time she'd thought she'd been unlucky enough to get the last cup in the pot, but now she wondered if it hadn't been pharmaceutically enhanced.

"I repeat. I'm not cheating." Lorna bit off the words, her jaw set.

"You've been coming here for a while. You walk away with about five grand every week. That's a cool quarter of a million a year—and that's just from my casino. How many others are you hitting?" His cool gaze raked her from head to foot, as if he wondered why she didn't dress better, taking in that kind of money.

Lorna felt her face getting hot, and that made her angry. She hadn't been embarrassed about anything in a very long time, embarrassment being a luxury she couldn't afford, but something about his assessment made her want to squirm. Okay, so she wasn't the best dresser in the world, but she was neat and clean, and that was what mattered. So what if she'd gotten her pants and short-sleeve blouse at Wal-Mart? She simply couldn't make herself spend a hundred dollars on a pair of shoes when a twelve-dollar pair fit her just as well. The eighty-eight dollar difference would buy a lot of food. And silk not only cost a lot, but it was difficult to care for; she would take a nice cotton/polyester blend, which didn't have to be ironed, over silk any day of the week.

"I said, how many other casinos are you hitting each week?"

"What I do isn't your business." She glared at him, glad for the anger and the surge of energy it gave her. Feeling angry was much better than feeling hurt. She wouldn't let this man's opinion matter enough to her that he could hurt her. Her clothes might be cheap, but they weren't ragged; she was clean, and she refused to be ashamed of them.

"On the contrary. I caught you. Therefore I should have Al warn the other security chiefs."

"You haven't *caught* me doing anything!" She was absolutely certain of that, because she hadn't *done* anything he could catch.

"You're lucky I'm the one in the driver's seat," he continued as if she hadn't spoken a word. "There's a certain element in Reno that thinks cheating is a crime deserving of capital punishment."

Her heartbeat stuttered. He was right, and she knew it. There were whispers on the street, tales of people who tried to tilt the odds their way—and who either disappeared completely or had assumed room temperature by the time they were found. She didn't have the blissful ignorance that would let her think he was merely exaggerating, because she had lived in the world where those things happened. She knew that world, knew the people who inhabited it. She had been careful to stay as invisible as possible, and she never used the ubiquitous players' cards that allowed the casinos to keep track of who was winning and who wasn't, but still she had done something wrong, something that called attention to herself. Her innocence wouldn't matter to some people; a word to the wrong person, and she was a dead woman.

Was he saying he didn't intend to turn her in, that he would keep the matter Inferno's private business?

Why would he do that? Only two possible reasons came to mind. One was the old sex-for-a-favor play: "Be nice to me, little girl, and I won't tell what I know." The other was that he might suspect her of cheating but had no evidence, and all he intended to do was maybe trick her into confessing or at the least bar her from the Inferno. If his reason was the former one, then he was a sleaze, and she knew how to deal with sleazes. If his reason was the latter, well, then he was a nice guy.

Which would be his tough luck.

He was watching her, really *watching* her, his

complete attention focused on reading every
flicker of emotion on her face. Lorna fought the
urge to fidget, but being the center of that sort of
concentration made her very uneasy. She preferred
to blend in with the crowd, to stay in the background; anonymity meant safety.

"Relax. I'm not going to blackmail you into
having sex with me—not that I'm not interested,"
he said, "but I don't need coercion to get sex when
I want it."

She almost jumped. Either he'd read her mind,
or she was getting really sloppy about guarding her
expression. She knew she wasn't sloppy; for too
long, her life had depended on staying sharp; the de-
fensive habits of a lifetime were deeply ingrained.
He'd read her mind. *Oh, God, he'd read her mind!*

Full-blown panic began to fog her mind; then it
immediately dissipated, forced out by a sharply
detailed image of the two of them having sex. For
a disorienting moment she felt as if she were
standing outside her own body, watching the two
of them in bed—naked, their bodies sweaty from
exertion, straining together. His muscled body bore
her down, crushing her into the tangled sheets.
Her arms and legs, pale against his olive-toned
skin, were wrapped around him. She smelled the
scents of sex and skin, felt the heat and weight of
him on top of her as he pushed slickly inside, heard

her own quick gasp as she lifted into his slow, controlled thrusts. She was about to climax, and so was he, his thrusts coming harder and faster—

She jerked herself away from the scenario, suddenly, horribly sure that if she let it carry on to the end she would humiliate herself by climaxing for real, right in front of him. She could barely keep herself in the present; the lure of even imagined pleasure was so strong that she wanted to go back, to lose herself in the dream, or hallucination, or whatever the hell it was.

Something was wrong. She wasn't in control of herself but instead was being tossed about by the weird eddies of power surging and retreating through the room. Neither could she get a handle on anything long enough to examine it; just when she thought she was grounded, she would get tossed into another reaction, another wild emotion bubbling to the surface.

He spoke again, seemingly oblivious to everything but his own thoughts. How could he not *feel* everything that was going on? Was she imagining everything? She clutched the arms of the chair, wondering if she was having some sort of mental breakdown.

"You're precognitive." He tilted his head as if he were studying an interesting specimen, a slight smile on his lips. "You're also a sensitive, and maybe there's a little bit of telekinesis thrown in. Interesting."

"Are you crazy?" she blurted, horrified, and still struggling to concentrate. *Interesting?* He was either on the verge of destroying her life or she was going crazy, and he thought it was *interesting?*

"I don't believe so. No, I'm fairly certain I'm sane." Amusement flickered in his eyes, warming them. "Go ahead, Lorna, make the leap. The only way I could know if you were a precog is…?" His voice trailed away on a questioning lilt, inviting her to finish the sentence.

She sat as if frozen, staring fixedly at him. Was he saying he really *could* read minds, or was he setting some trap she couldn't yet see?

A sudden, freezing cold swept through the room, so cold she ached down to the bone, and with it came that same overwhelming sense of dread she'd felt when she'd first entered the room and seen him. Lorna hugged herself and set her teeth to keep them from chattering. She wanted to run and couldn't; her muscles simply wouldn't obey the instinct to flee.

Was he the source of this…this *turmoil* in the room? She couldn't put a better description to it than that, because she'd never felt quite this way before, as if reality had become layered with hallucinations.

"You can relax. There's no way I can prove it, so I can't charge you with cheating. But I knew what you are as soon as you said you thought I was 'doing it.' Doing what? You didn't say, but the statement was an intriguing one, because it meant you're sensitive to the currents in the room." He steepled his fingers and tapped them against his lips, regarding her over them with an unwavering gaze. "Normal people would never have felt a thing. A lot of times, one form of psi ability goes hand in hand with other forms, so it's obvious, now, how you win so consistently. You know what card will turn up, don't you? You know which slot machines will pay off. Maybe you can even manipulate the computer to give you three in a row."

The cold left the room as abruptly as it had entered. She had been tensed to resist it, and the sudden lessening of pressure made her feel as if she might fall out of the chair. Lorna clenched her jaw tight, afraid to say anything. She couldn't let herself be drawn into a discussion about paranormal abilities. For all she knew, he had this room wired for both video and audio and was recording everything. What if one of those weird hallucinations seized control of her again? She might say whatever he wanted her to say, admit to any wild charge. Heck— everything she was feeling might be the result of some weird special effects he'd installed.

"I know you aren't Raintree," he continued softly. "I know my own. So the big question is…are you Ansara, or are you just a stray?"

Shock rescued her once again. "A *stray?*" she echoed, jerking back into a world that felt real. There was still an underlying sense of disorientation, but at least that sexually disturbing image was gone, the cold was gone, the dread was gone.

She took a deep breath and fought down the hot rush of anger. He'd just compared her to an unwanted mongrel. Beneath the anger, though, was the corrosive edge of old, bitter despair. *Unwanted.* She'd always been that. For a while, a wondrously sweet moment, she had thought that would change, but then even that last hope had been taken from her, and she didn't have the heart, the will, to try again. Something inside her had given up, but the pain hadn't dulled.

He made a dismissive gesture. "Not that kind of stray. We use it to describe a person of ability who is unaffiliated."

"Unaffiliated with *what?* What are you talking about?" Her bewilderment on this point, at least, was real.

"Someone who is neither Raintree nor Ansara."

His explanations were going in circles, and so were her thoughts. Frustrated, frightened, she made a sharp motion with her hand and snapped, "Who in hell is Aunt Sarah?"

Tilting his head back, he burst out laughing, the sound quick and easy, as if he did it a lot. The pit of her stomach fluttered. Imagining sex with him had lowered defenses she usually kept raised high, and the distant acknowledgment of his attractiveness had become a full-fledged awareness. Against her will she noticed the muscular lines of his throat, the sculpted line of his jaw. He was… *Handsome* was, in an odd way, too feminine a word to describe him. He was *striking*, his features altogether too compelling to be merely handsome. Nor were his looks the first thing she'd noticed about him; by far her first impression had been one of power.

"Not 'Aunt Sarah,' " he said, still laughing. "Ansara. A-N-S-A-R-A."

"I've never heard of them," she said warily, wondering if this was some type of mob thing he was talking about. She didn't suffer from the delusion that organized crime was restricted to the old Italian families in New York and Chicago.

"Haven't you?" He said it pleasantly enough, but with her nerve-endings stripped raw the way they were, she felt the doubt—and the inherent threat—as clearly as if he'd shouted at her.

She had to get her reactions under control. The weird stuff happening in this room had taken her by surprise, shocked her into a vulnerability she normally didn't allow, but now that she'd had a moment without any new assault on her senses, she began to get her composure back. Mentally she reassembled her internal barriers; it was a struggle, because concentration was difficult, but grimly she persisted. She might not know what was going on, but she knew protecting herself was vitally important.

He was waiting for her to respond to his rhetorical question, but she ignored him and focused on her shields—

Shields?

Where had that word come from? She never thought of herself as having shields. She thought of herself as strong, her heart weathered and toughened by hard times; she thought of herself as unemotional.

She never thought of herself as having *shields*.

Until now.

She was the most unshielded sensitive he'd ever seen, Dante thought as he watched her struggle against the flow and surge of power. She reacted like a complete novice to both his thoughts and his affinity for fire. He had his gift under strict control now, but to test her, he'd sent tiny blasts of it into the room, making the candles dance. She'd latched on to the arms of the chair as if she needed to anchor herself, her alarmed gaze darting around as if searching for monsters.

When he'd picked up on her expectation of

being blackmailed for sex—which hadn't exactly been hard to guess—he'd allowed himself a brief, pleasant little fantasy, to which she'd responded as if he'd really had her naked in bed. Her mouth had gotten red and soft, her cheeks flushed, her eyes heavy-lidded, while beneath that cheap sweater her nipples had become so hard their shape had been visible even through her bra.

Damn. For a moment there, she'd been in real danger of the fantasy becoming fact.

She might be Ansara, but if she was, she was completely untutored. Either that or she was skilled enough to *appear* untutored. If she *was* Ansara, he would bet on the latter. Being Raintree had a lot of advantages and one big disadvantage: an implacable enemy. The hostility between the two clans had erupted into a huge pitched battle about two hundred years ago, and the Raintree had been victorious, the Ansara almost destroyed. The tattered remnants of the once-powerful clan were scattered around the world and had never recovered to the point that they could again make concerted war on the Raintree, but that didn't mean that the occasional lone Ansara didn't try to make trouble for them.

Like the Raintree, the Ansara had different gifts of varying degrees of strength. The ones Dante had infrequently crossed paths with had all been trained as well as any Raintree, which meant none of them were to be taken lightly. While they weren't the threat they had been before, he was always aware that any one of them would love a chance to get at him in any way.

It would be just like an Ansara to get a kick out of stealing from him. There were bigger casinos in Reno, but stealing from the Inferno would be **a** huge feather in her cap—*if* she was Ansara.

He had some empathic ability—nothing in the same ballpark as his younger sister, Mercy, but enough that he could read most people as soon as he touched them. The exceptions, mainly, were the Ansara, because they had been trained to shield themselves in a way normal humans never were. Sensitives *had* to shield or be overwhelmed by the forces around them...much as Lorna Clay seemed to have been overwhelmed.

Maybe she was just a good actress.

The candlelight was magic on her skin, in her hair. She was a pretty woman, with finely molded bone structure, if a tad brittle and hostile in her attitude, but what the hell—if he'd been caught cheating, he would probably be hostile, too.

He wanted to touch her, to see if he could read anything.

She would probably run screaming from the room if he laid a hand on her, though. She was so tightly wound that she might throw herself backward in the chair if he said "Boo!" He thought about doing it, just for the amusement value.

He would have, if not for the very serious matter of cheating.

He leaned forward to hammer home a point, and—

A loud but not unpleasant tone sounded, followed by another, then another. A burst of adrenaline shot through his system, and he was on his feet, grabbing her arm and hauling her out of the chair before the recorded announcement could begin.

"What is it?" she cried, her face going white, but she didn't try to pull away from him.

"Fire," he said briefly, all but dragging her to the door. Once the fire alarm sounded all the elevators stopped responding to calls—and they were on the nineteenth floor.

Chapter 4

Lorna stumbled and almost went down on one knee as he dragged her through the doorway. Her hip banged painfully into the door frame; then she regained her balance, lurched upward and hurtled through so fast that she immediately crashed into the wall on the other side. Her arm, held tight in his iron grip, was wrenched as he ruthlessly pulled her onward. She didn't say a word, didn't cry out, almost didn't even notice the pain, because the living nightmare she was in crowded out everything else.

Fire!

She saw him give her a searing, comprehensive look; then he released her arm and instead clamped his left arm around her waist, locking her to his side and holding her up as he ran toward the stairs. They were alone in the hallway, but as soon as he opened the door marked Exit, she could hear the thunder of footsteps below them as people stampeded down the stairs.

The air in the hallway had been clear, but as the door clanged shut behind them, she smelled it: the throat-burning stench of smoke. Her heartbeat stuttered. She was afraid of fire, always had been, and it wasn't just the caution of an intelligent person. If she had to pick the worst way on earth to die, it would be by fire. She had nightmares about being trapped behind a wall of flame, unable to get to someone—a child, maybe?—who was more important to her than her own life, or even to save herself. Just as the flames reached her and she felt her flesh begin to sear, she would wake, trembling and in tears from the horror.

She didn't like any open flame—candles, fireplaces, or even gas cooktops. Now Dante Raintree was carrying her down into the heart of the beast, when every instinct she had screamed for her to go up, up into fresh air, as far away from fire as she could get.

As they made the turn at the first landing, the mental chaos of panic began to strengthen and grab at her, and she fought it back. Logically she knew they had to go down, that jumping off the roof wasn't a viable option. Clenching her teeth together to keep them from chattering, she concentrated on keeping her balance, making sure her feet hit each step squarely, though the way he was holding her, she doubted she could stumble. She didn't want to impede him or, God forbid, cause both of them to fall.

They caught up with a knot of people also going down the stairs, but the passage was clogged, and people were shouting at others to move out of the way. The uproar was confusing; no one could make themselves understood, and some were coughing now as the smoke thickened.

"You can't go up!" Raintree thundered, his voice booming over the pushing, yelling human logjam, and only then did Lorna realize that the uproar was caused by people trying to push their way up the stairs while others were just as focused on going down.

"Who the hell are you?" someone bellowed from below.

"The owner of the Inferno, that's who the hell I am," Raintree snapped. "I built this casino, and I know where I'm going. Now turn your ass around and go all the way down to the ground floor, that's the only way out."

"The smoke's worse that way!"

"Then take off your shirt and tie it over your nose and mouth. Everyone do that," he ordered, booming out the words again so all could hear him. He suited action to words, releasing Lorna to strip out of his expensive suit jacket. She stood numbly beside him, watching as he swiftly removed a knife from his pocket, flicked it open, and sliced the gray silk lining from the jacket. Then he just as swiftly ripped the lining into two oblong panels. Handing one panel to her, he said, "Use this," as he closed the knife and slipped it back into his pocket.

She expected some of the group to push on upstairs, regardless of what he said, but no one did. Instead, several men, the ones who wore jackets, were following his example and ripping out the garments' linings. Others were taking off their shirts, tearing them up and offering pieces to women who were reluctant to remove their blouses. Lorna hastily tied the silk over her nose and mouth, pulling it tight so it hugged her face like a surgical mask. Beside her, Raintree was doing the same.

"Go!" he ordered, and like obedient sheep, they did. The tangle of people began to unravel, then ribbon downward. Lorna found her own feet moving as if they weren't attached to her, taking her down, down, closer to whatever living, crackling hell awaited them. Every cell in her body was screaming in protest, her breath was coming in strangled gasps, but still she kept going down the stairs as if she had no will of her own.

His hand put pressure on her waist, moving her to one side. "Let us pass," he said. "I'll show you the way out." The people in front of them all moved to one side, and though Lorna heard several angry mutters, they were drowned out by others telling the mutterers to shut up, that it was his place and he'd know how to get out of the building.

More and more people were crowding into the stairwell ahead of them as the floors emptied, but they pressed to the side as Raintree moved Lorna and himself past them. The acrid smoke stung her eyes, making them water, and she could feel the temperature rising as they went down. How many floors had they descended? At the next landing she peered at the door and the number painted on it, but the tears in her eyes blurred the figures. Sixteen, maybe. Or fifteen. Was that all? Hadn't they gone farther than that? She tried to remember how many landings they had passed, but she had been too numb with terror to pay attention.

She was going to die in this building. She could feel the icy breath of Death as it waited for her, just on the other side of the flames that she couldn't see but could nevertheless feel, as if they were a great force pulling at her. *This* was why she had always been so afraid of fire; she had somehow known she was destined to burn. Soon she would be gone, her life force seared or choked away—

—and no one would miss her.

Dante kept everyone moving downward, the mind compulsion he was using forcing them into an orderly evacuation. He had never tried this particular power, never even known he possessed it, and if they hadn't been so close to the summer solstice, he doubted he could have done it. Hell, he hadn't been sure he could make it work at all, much less on such a large group, but with fire threatening to destroy the casino he'd worked so hard to build, he'd poured all his will into the thought, into his words, and they had obeyed.

He could feel the flames singing their siren song, calling to him. Maybe they were even feeding his power, because the close proximity of fire was making his heart rate soar as adrenaline poured through him. Even though smoke was stinging his eyes and filtering through the silk tied over his nose and mouth, he felt so alive that his skin could barely contain him. He wanted to laugh, wanted to throw his arms wide and invite the fire to come to him, to do battle with him, so he could exert his will over it as he did over these people.

If it hadn't been for the level of concentration he needed to keep the mind compulsion in place, he would already have been mentally joined in battle. Everything in him yearned for the struggle. He *would* vanquish the flames, but first he had to get these people to safety.

Lorna kept pace beside him, but a quick glance at her face—what he could see of it above the gray silk—told him that only his will was keeping her going down the stairs. She was paper white, and her eyes were almost blank with terror. He pulled her closer to his side, wanting her within reach when they got to the ground floor, because otherwise her panic might be strong enough that she could break free of the compulsion and bolt. And he wasn't finished with her yet. In fact, with this damn fire, he thought he might have a good deal more to discuss with her than cheating at blackjack.

If she was Ansara, if she had somehow been involved in starting the fire, she would die. It was that simple.

He'd touched her, but he couldn't tell if she was Ansara or not. His empathic power was on the wimpy side anyway, and right now he couldn't really concentrate on reading her. Not picking up anything meant she was either a stray or she was Ansara, and strong enough to shield her real self from him. Either way, the matter would have to wait.

The smoke was getting thicker, but not drastically so. There was some talking, though for the most part people were saving their breath for getting down the stairs. There was, however, a steady barrage of coughing.

The fire, he sensed, was concentrated so far in the casino, but it was rapidly spreading toward the hotel portion of the building. Unlike most hotel/casinos, which were built in such a way that the guests were forced to walk through the casino on their way to anywhere else, thereby increasing the probability that they would stop and play, Dante had built Inferno with the guest rooms off to one side. There was a common area where the two joined and overlapped, but he also provided a bit of distance for the guest who wanted it. He'd been taking a chance, but the design had worked out. By concentrating on providing a level of elegance unmatched at any other hotel/casino in Reno, he'd made Inferno different and therefore desirable.

That offset design would save a lot of lives tonight. The guests who had been in the casino, though…he didn't know about them. Nor could he let himself dwell on them, or he might lose control of the people in the stairwell. He couldn't help the people in the casino, at least not now, so he let himself think only about his immediate charges. If these people panicked, if they started pushing and running, not only would some people fall and be trampled, but the crowd might well crush the exit bar and prevent the door from being opened. That had happened before, and would happen again—but not in his place, not if he could help it.

They reached another landing, and he peered through the smoke at the number on the door. Three. Just two more floors, thank God. The smoke was getting so thick that his lungs were burning. "We're almost there," he said, to keep the people behind him focused, and he heard people begin repeating the words to those stacked on the stairs above them.

He wrapped his arm around Lorna's waist and clamped her to his side, lifting her off her feet as he descended the remaining floors two steps at a time. The door opened not to the outside but into a corridor lined with offices. He held the door open with his body, and as people stumbled into the corridor, he said, "Turn right. Go through the double doors at the end of the hall, turn right again, and the door just past the soda machines will open onto the ground level of the parking deck. Go, go, go!"

They went, propelled by his will—stumbling and coughing, but moving nevertheless. The air here was thick and hot, his vision down to only a few feet, and the people who scrambled past him looked like ghosts and disappeared in seconds. Only their coughing and the sound of their footsteps marked their progress.

He felt Lorna move, trying to break his grip, trying to obey not only his mental command but the commands of her own panic-stricken brain. He tightened his hold on her. Maybe he could fine-tune the compulsion enough to exclude her right now…. No, it wasn't worth the risk. While he had them all under his control, he kept them there and kept them moving. All he had to do was hold Lorna to keep her from escaping.

He could feel the fire at his back. Not literally, but closer now, much closer. Everything in him yearned to turn and engage with the force of nature that was his to call and control, his to own. Not yet. *Not yet…*

Then no more smoke-shrouded figures were emerging from the stairwell, and with Lorna firmly in his grip he turned to the left—away from the parking deck and safety, and toward the roaring red demon.

"*Noooo.*"

The sound was little more than a moan, and she bucked like a wild thing in the circle of his arm. Hastily he gave one last mental shove at the stream of people headed toward the parking deck, then transferred the compulsion to a different command, this one directed solely at Lorna: "Stay with me."

Immediately she stopped struggling, though he could hear the strangled, panicked sounds she was making as he strode through the smoke to another door, one that opened into the lobby.

He threw the door open and stepped into hell, dragging her with him.

The sprinkler system was making a valiant effort, spraying water down on the lobby, but the heat was a monster furnace that evaporated the spray before it reached the floor. It blasted them like a shock wave, a physical blow, but he muttered a curse and pushed back. Because they were produced by the fire, were parts of the fire, he owned the heat and smoke as surely as he owned the flames. Now that he could concentrate, he deflected them, creating a protective bubble, a force field, around Lorna and himself that sent the smoke swirling and held the heat at bay, protecting them.

The casino was completely engaged. The flames were greedy tongues of red, great sheets of orange and black, transparent forks of gold, that danced and roared in their eagerness to consume everything within reach. Several of the elegant white columns had already ignited like huge torches, and the vast expanse of carpet was a sea of small fires, lit by the falling debris.

The columns were acting as candles, wicking the flames upward to the ceiling. He started there, pulling power from deep inside and using it to bend the fire to his will. Slowly, slowly, the flames licking up the columns began to die down, vanquished by a superior force.

Doing that much, while maintaining the bubble of protection around them, took every ounce of power he had. Something wasn't right. He realized that even as he concentrated on the columns, feeling the strain deep inside. His head began to hurt; killing the flames shouldn't take this much effort. They were slow in responding to his command, but he didn't let up even as he wondered if the energy he'd used on the group mind compulsion had somehow drained him. He didn't feel as if it had, but something was definitely wrong.

When only tendrils of smoke were coming from the columns, he switched his attention to the walls, pushing back, pushing back....

Out of the corner of his eye, he saw the columns burst into flame again.

With a roar of fury and disbelief, he blasted his will at the flames, and they subsided once again.

What the hell?

Windows exploded, sending shards of glass flying in all directions. Brutal streams of water poured through from the front, courtesy of the Reno Fire

Department, but the flames seemed to give a hoarse laugh before roaring back brighter and hotter than before. One of the two huge, glittering crystal chandeliers pulled loose from the fire-weakened ceiling and crashed to the floor, throwing up a glittering spray of lethal glass splinters. They were far enough away that few of the splinters reached them, but one of the lovely crystal hornets stung his cheek, sending a rivulet of blood running down his face. Maybe they should have ducked, he thought with distant humor.

He could feel Lorna pressed against him, shaking convulsively and making little keening sounds of terror, but she was helpless to break the mind compulsion he'd put on her. Had any of the glass hit her? No time to check. With a great whoosh, a huge tongue of fire rolled across the ceiling overhead, consuming everything in its path as well as what felt like most of the available oxygen; then it began eating its way down the wall behind them, sealing off any escape.

Mentally, he pushed at the flames, willing them to retreat, calling on all his reserves of strength and power. He was the Dranir of the Raintree; the fire *would* obey him.

Except it didn't.

Instead it began crawling across the carpet, small fires combining into larger ones, and those joining with others until the floor was ablaze, getting closer, closer....

He couldn't control it. He had never before met a flame he couldn't bend to his will, but this was something beyond his power. Using the mind compulsion that way must have weakened him somehow; it wasn't something he'd done before, so he didn't know what the ramifications were. Well, yeah, he did; unless a miracle happened, the ramifications in this case were two deaths: his and Lorna's.

He refused to accept that. He'd never given up, never let a fire beat him; he wouldn't start with this one.

The bubble of protection wavered, letting smoke filter in. Lorna began coughing convulsively, struggling against his grip even though she wouldn't be able to run unless he released her from the compulsion. There was nowhere to run *to*, anyway.

Grimly, he faced the flames. He needed more power. He had thrown everything he had left at the fire, and it wasn't enough. If Gideon or Mercy were here, they could link with him, combine strengths, but that sort of partnership required close proximity, so he had only himself to rely on. There was no other source of power for him to tap—

—except for Lorna.

He didn't ask; he didn't take the time to warn

her what he was going to do; he simply wrapped both arms around her from behind and blasted his way past her mental shields, ruthlessly taking what he needed. Relief poured through him at what he found. Yes, she had power, more than he'd expected. He didn't stop to analyze what kind of power she had, because it didn't matter; on this level, power was power, like electricity. Different machines could take the same power and do wildly different things, like vacuuming the floor or playing music. It was the same principle. She had power; he took it, and used it to bolster his own gift.

She gave a thin scream and bucked in his arms, then went rigid.

Furiously he attacked the flames, sending out a 360-degree mental blast that literally blew out the wall of fire behind him and took the physical wall with it, as well. The rush of renewed oxygen made the fire in front of him flare, so he gathered himself and did it again, pouring even more energy into the battle, feeling his own reserves well up, renewed, as he took every ounce of power and strength from Lorna and blended it with his own.

His entire body was tingling, his muscles burning with the effort it took to contain and focus. The invisible bubble of protection around them began to shimmer and took on a faint glow. Sweating, swearing, ignoring the pain in his head, he blasted the energy of his will at the fire again and again, beating it back even while he tried to calculate how long he'd been standing there, how much time he needed to give the people in the hotel to escape. There were multiple stairwells, and he was certain not all evacuations had been as orderly as the one he'd controlled. Was everyone out by now? What about disabled people? They would have to be helped down the flights of stairs. If he stopped, the fire would surge forward, engulfing the hotel—so he couldn't stop. Until the fire was controlled, he couldn't stop.

He couldn't put it out, not completely. For whatever reason, whether he was depleted or distracted or the fire itself was somehow different, he couldn't put it out. He accepted that now. All he could do was hold the flames at bay until the fire department had them under control.

That was what he concentrated on, controlling the fire instead of extinguishing it. That conserved his energy, and he needed every bit he had, because the fierceness of the fire never stopped pushing back, never stopped struggling for freedom. Time meant nothing, because no matter how long it took, no matter how his head hurt, he had to endure.

Somewhere along the way he lost the line of division between himself and the fire. It was an enemy, but it was beautiful in its destruction; it danced for him as always, magic in its movement and colors. He felt its beauty like molten lava running through his veins, felt his body respond with mindless lust until his erection strained painfully against his zipper. Lorna had to feel it, but there wasn't a damned thing he could do to make it go away. The best he could do, under the circumstances, was not grind it against her.

Finally, hoarse shouts intruded through the diminished roar of the beast. Turning his head slightly, Dante saw teams of firefighters advancing with their hoses. Quickly he let the bubble of protection dissolve, leaving him and Lorna exposed to the smoke and heat.

With his first breath, the hot smoke seared all the way down to his lungs. He choked, coughed, tried to draw another breath. Lorna sagged to her knees, and he dropped down beside her as the first firefighters reached them.

Chapter 5

Lorna sat on the bumper of a fire-medic truck and clutched a scratchy blanket around her. The night was warm, but she was soaking wet, and she couldn't seem to stop shivering. She'd heard the fire medic say she wasn't in shock; though her blood pressure was a little high, which was understandable, her pulse rate was near normal. She was just chilled from being wet.

And, yet, everything around her seemed…muted, as if there were a glass wall between her and the rest of the world. Her mind felt numb, barely able to function. When the medic had asked her name, for the life of her, she hadn't been able to remember,

much less articulate it. But she *had* remembered
that she never brought a purse to a casino because
of thieves and that she kept her money in one
pocket and her driver's license in another, so she'd
pulled out her license and showed it to him. It was
a Missouri license, because she hadn't gotten a license here. To get a Nevada license, you had to be
a resident and gainfully employed. It was the "gainfully employed" part that tripped her up.

"Are you Lorna Clay?" the medic had asked,
and she'd nodded.

"Does your throat hurt?" he'd asked then, and
that seemed as reasonable an explanation for her
continued silence as any other, so she'd nodded
again. He'd looked at her throat, seemed briefly
puzzled, then given her oxygen to breathe. She
should be checked out at the hospital, he'd said.

Yeah, right. She had no intention of going to a
hospital. The only place she wanted to go was *away*.

And, yet, she remained right where she was
while Raintree was checked out. There was blood
on his face, but the cut turned out to be small. She
heard him tell the medics he was fine, that, no, he
didn't think he was burned anywhere, that they'd
been very lucky.

Lucky, her ass. The thought was as clear as a
bell, rising from the sluggish morass that was her
brain. He'd held her there in the middle of that

roaring hell for what felt like an eternity. They should be crispy critters. They should, at least, be gasping for breath through damaged airways, instead of being *fine*. She knew what fire did. She'd seen it, she'd smelled it, and it was ugly. It destroyed everything in its path. What it didn't do was dance all around and leave you unscathed.

Yet, here she was—unscathed. Relatively, anyway. She felt as if she'd been run over by a truck, but at least she wasn't burned.

She should have been burned. She should have been *dead*. Whenever she contemplated the fact that she not only wasn't dead, she wasn't even injured, her head ached so much she could barely stand to breathe, and the glass wall between her and reality got a little bit thicker. So she didn't think about being alive, or dead or anything else. She just sat there while the nightmarish scene revolved around her, lights flashing, crowds of people milling about, the firefighters still busy with their hoses putting out the remaining flames and making certain they didn't flare again. The fire engines rumbled so loudly that the noise wore on her, made her want to cover her ears, but she didn't do that, either. She just waited.

For what, she wasn't certain. She should leave. She thought a hundred times about just walking away into the night, but putting thought into action proved impossible. No matter how much she wanted to leave, she was bound by an inertia she couldn't seem to fight. All she could do was...sit.

Then Raintree stood, and, abruptly, she found herself standing, too, levered upward by some impulse she didn't understand. She just knew that if he was standing, she would stand. She was too mentally exhausted to come up with any reason that made more sense.

His face was so black with soot that only the whites of his eyes showed, so she figured she must look pretty much the same. Great. That meant she didn't have much chance of being able to slip away unnoticed. He took a cloth someone offered him and swiped it over his sooty face, which didn't do much good. Soot was oily; anything other than soap just sort of moved it around.

Determination in his stride, he moved toward a small clump of policemen, three uniforms and two plainclothes. Vague alarm rose in Lorna. Was he going to turn her in? Without any proof? She desperately wanted to hang back, but, instead, she found herself docilely following him.

Why was she doing this? Why wasn't she leaving? She struggled with the questions, trying to get her brain to function. He hadn't even glanced in her direction; he wouldn't have any idea where she'd gone if she dropped back now and sort of blended in with the crowd—as much as she could blend in anywhere, covered with soot the way she was. But others also showed the effects of the smoke; some of the casino employees, for instance, and the players. She probably could have slipped away, if she felt capable of making the effort.

Why was her brain so sluggish? On a very superficial level, her thought processes seemed to be normal, but below that was nothing but sludge. There was something important she should remember, something that briefly surfaced just long enough to cause a niggle of worry, then disappeared like a wisp of smoke. She frowned, trying to pull the memory out, but the effort only intensified the pain in her head, and she stopped.

Raintree approached the two plainclothes cops and introduced himself. Lorna tried to make herself inconspicuous, which might be a losing cause considering how she looked, plus the fact that she was standing only a few feet away. They all eyed her with the mixture of suspicion and curiosity cops just seemed to have. Her heart started pounding. What would she do if Raintree accused her of cheating? Run? Look at him as if he were an idiot? Maybe *she* was the idiot, standing there like a sacrificial lamb.

The image galvanized her as nothing else had. She would *not* be a willing victim. She tried to take a step away, but for some reason the action seemed beyond her. All she wanted to do was stay with him.

Stay with me.

The words resonated through her tired brain, making her head ache. Wearily, she rubbed her forehead, wondering where she'd heard the words and why they mattered.

"Where were you when the fire started, Mr. Raintree?" one of the detectives asked. He and the other detective had introduced themselves, but their names had flown out of Lorna's head as soon as she'd heard them.

"In my office, talking to Ms. Clay." He indicated Lorna without really looking in her direction, as if he knew just where she was standing.

They looked at her more sharply now; then the detective who had been talking to Raintree said, "My partner will take her statement while I'm taking yours, so we can save time."

Sure, Lorna thought sarcastically. She had some beachfront property here in Reno she wanted to sell, too. The detectives wanted to separate her from Raintree so she couldn't hear what he said and they couldn't coordinate their statements. If a business was going down the tubes, sometimes the owner tried to minimize losses by burning it down and collecting on the insurance policy.

The other detective stepped to her side. Raintree glanced at her over his shoulder. "Don't go far. I don't want to lose you in this crowd."

What was he up to? she wondered. He'd made it sound as if they were in a relationship or something. But when the detective said, "Let's walk over here," Lorna obediently walked beside him for about twenty feet, then abruptly stopped as if she couldn't take one step more.

"Here," she said, surprised at how raspy and weak her voice was. She had coughed some, sure, but her voice sounded as if she'd been hacking for days. She was barely audible over all the noise from the fire engines.

"Sure." The detective looked around, casually positioning himself so that Lorna had to stand with her back to Raintree. "I'm Detective Harvey. Your name is…"

"Lorna Clay." At least she remembered her name this time, though for a horrible split second she hadn't been certain. She rubbed her forehead again, wishing this confounded headache would go away.

"Do you live here?"

"For the moment. I haven't decided if I'll stay." She knew she wouldn't. She never stayed in one place for very long. A few months, six at the most, and she moved on. He asked for her address, and she rattled it off. If he ran a check on her, he would find the most grievous thing against her was a speeding ticket she'd received three years ago. She'd paid the fine without argument; no problem there. So long as Raintree didn't bring a charge of cheating against her, she was fine. She wanted to look over her shoulder at him but knew better than to appear nervous or, even worse, as if she were checking with him on what answers to give.

"Where were you when the fire started?"

He'd just heard Raintree, when asked the identical question, say he'd been with her, but that was how cops operated. "I don't know when the fire started," she said, a tad irritably. "I was in Mr. Raintree's office when the alarm sounded."

"What time was that?"

"I don't have a watch on. I don't know. I wouldn't have thought to check the time, anyway. Fire scares the bejesus out of me."

One corner of his mouth twitched a little, but he disciplined it. He had a nice, lived-in sort of face, a little droopy at the jowls, wrinkly around the eyes. "That's okay. We can get the time from the security system. How long had you been with Mr. Raintree when the alarm sounded?"

Now, there was a question. Lorna thought back to the episodes of panic she'd experienced in that office, to the confusing hallucinations, or whatever the disconcerting sexual fantasy was. *Nothing* in that room had been normal, and though she usually had a good grasp of time, she found herself unable to even estimate. "I don't know. It was sunset when I went in. That's all I can tell you."

He made a note of her answer. God only knew what he thought they'd been doing, she thought wearily, but she couldn't bring herself to care.

"What did you do when the fire alarm sounded?"

"We ran for the stairs."

"What floor were you on?"

Now, that, she knew, because she'd watched the numbers on the ride up in the elevator. "The nineteenth."

He made a note of that, too. Lorna thought to herself that if she intended to burn a building down she wouldn't go to the nineteenth floor to wait for the alarm. Raintree hadn't had anything to do with whatever had caused the fire, but the cops had to check out everything or they wouldn't be doing their jobs. Though…did detectives normally go to the scene of a fire? A fire inspector or fire marshal, whichever Reno had, would have to determine that a fire was caused by arson before they treated it as a crime.

"What happened then?"

"There were a lot of people in the stairwell," she said slowly, trying to get the memory to form. "I remember…a lot of people. We could go only a couple of floors before everyone got jammed up, because some of the people from the lower floors were trying to go up." The smoke had been heavy, too, because visibility had been terrible, people passing by like ghosts… No. That had been later. There hadn't been a lot of smoke in the stairs right then. Later— She wasn't certain about later. The sequence of events was all jumbled up, and she couldn't seem to sort everything out.

"Go on," Detective Harvey prompted when she was silent for several moments.

"Mr. Raintree told them—the people coming up the stairs—they'd have to go back, there was no way out if they kept going up."

"Did they argue?"

"No, they all turned around. No one panicked." Except her. She'd barely been able to breathe, and it hadn't been because of the smoke. The memory was becoming clearer, and she was amazed at how orderly the evacuation had been. No one had pushed; no one had been running. People had been hurrying, of course, but not being so reckless that they risked a nasty fall. In retrospect, their behavior had been damned unnatural. How could everyone have been so calm? Didn't they know what fire *did*?

But she hadn't run, either, she realized. She hadn't pushed. She had gone at a steady pace, held to Raintree's side by his arm.

Wait. Had he been holding her then? She didn't think he had been. He'd touched her waist, sort of guiding her along, but she'd been free to run. So...why hadn't she?

She had trooped along like everyone else, in an orderly line. Inside she'd been screaming, but outwardly she'd been controlled.

Controlled... Not self-controlled, but controlled like a puppet, as if she hadn't had a will of her own. Her mind had been screaming at her to run, but her body simply hadn't obeyed.

"Ms. Clay?"

Lorna felt her breath start coming faster as she relived those moments. Fire! Coming closer and closer, she didn't want to go, she wanted to run, but she couldn't. She was caught in one of those nightmares when you try to run but can't, when you try to scream but can't make a sound—

"Ms. Clay?"

"I— What?" Dazed, she stared up at him. From the mixture of impatience and concern on his face, she thought he must have called her name several times.

"What did you do when you got out?"

Shuddering, she gathered herself. "We didn't. I mean, we got to the ground floor and Mr. Raintree sent the others to the right, toward the parking deck. Then he...we..." Her voice faltered. She had been fighting him, trying to follow the others;

she remembered that. Then he'd said, "*Stay with me,*" and she had, with no will to do otherwise, even though she'd been half mad with terror.

Stay with me.

When he'd sat, she'd sat. When he'd stood, she'd stood. When he'd moved, that was when she had moved. Until then, she had been incapable of taking a single step away from him.

Just moments ago he'd said, "Don't go far," and she'd been able to leave his side then—but she hadn't gone far before she'd stopped as if she'd hit a brick wall.

A horrible suspicion began to grow. He was controlling her somehow, maybe with some kind of posthypnotic suggestion, though when and how he'd hypnotized her, she had no idea. All sorts of weird things had been happening in his office. Maybe those damn candles had actually given off some kind of gas that had drugged her.

"Go on," said Detective Harvey, breaking into her thoughts.

"We went to the left," she said, beginning to shake. She wrapped her arms around herself, hugging the blanket close in an effort to control her wayward muscles, but in seconds, she was trembling from head to foot. "Into the lobby. The fire—" The fire had leaped at them like a maddened beast, roaring with delight. The heat had been searing for the tiniest fraction of a second. She'd been choking on the smoke. Then…no smoke, no heat. Both had just gone away. She and Raintree should have been overcome in seconds, but they hadn't been. She'd been able to breathe. She hadn't felt the heat, even though she'd watched the tongues of fire hungrily lapping across the carpet toward her. "The fire sort of *w-whooshed* across the ceiling and got behind us, and we were trapped."

"Would you like to sit down?" he asked, interrupting his line of questioning, but considering how violently she was shaking, he probably thought sitting her down before she fell down was a good idea.

She might have thought so, too, if sitting down hadn't meant sitting on asphalt littered with the debris of a fire and running with streams of sooty water. He probably meant sit down somewhere else, which she would have liked, if she'd felt capable of moving a single step beyond where she was right now. She shook her head. "I'm okay, just wet and cold and shaken up some." If there was an award given out for massive understatement, she'd just won it.

He eyed her for a moment, then evidently decided she knew whether or not she needed to sit down. He'd tried, anyway, which relieved him of any obligation. "What did you do?"

Better not to tell him she'd felt surrounded by

some sort of force field; this wasn't *Star Wars*, so he might not understand. Better not to tell him she'd felt a cool breeze in her hair. She must have been drugged; there was no other explanation.

"There wasn't anything we *could* do. We were trapped. I remember Mr. Raintree swearing a blue streak. I remember choking and being on the floor. Then the firefighters got to us and brought us out." In the interest of believability, she had heavily condensed the night's events as she remembered them, but, surely, they couldn't have been in the lobby for very long, no more than thirty seconds. An imaginary force field couldn't have held off real heat and smoke. The firefighters must have been close to them all along, but she'd been too panic-stricken to notice.

There was something else, probably that worrisome niggle of memory, that she couldn't quite grasp. Something else had happened. She knew it; she just couldn't think what it was. Maybe after she showered and washed her hair—several times—and got twenty or thirty hours of sleep, she might remember.

Detective Harvey glanced over her shoulder then flipped his little notebook shut. "You're lucky to be alive. Have you been checked for smoke inhalation?"

"Yes, I'm okay." The medic had been puzzled by her good condition, but she didn't tell the detective that.

"I imagine Mr. Raintree will be tied up here for quite a while, but you're free to go. Do you have a number where you can be reached if we have any further questions for you?"

She started to ask, *Like what?* but instead said, "Sure," and gave him her cell-phone number.

"That local?"

"It's my cell." Now that cell numbers could be transferred, she no longer bothered with a landline so long as she had cell-phone service wherever she temporarily settled.

"Got a local number?"

"No, that's it. Sorry. I didn't see any point in getting a landline unless I decided to stay."

"No problem. Thanks for your cooperation." He nodded a brief acknowledgment at her.

Because it seemed the thing to do, Lorna managed a faint smile for him as he strolled back to the other detective, but it quickly faded. She was exhausted and filthy. Her head hurt. Now that Detective Harvey had finished interviewing her, she was going home.

She tried. She made several attempts to walk away, but for some reason she couldn't make her feet move. Frustration grew in her. She had walked over here a few minutes ago, so there was no reason why she shouldn't be able to walk now. Just to see if she could move at all, without turning around, she stepped back, moving closer to Raintree. No problem. All her parts worked just as they should.

Experimentally, she took a step forward, and heaved a sigh of relief when her feet and legs actually obeyed. She was beyond exhausted if the simple act of walking had become so complicated. Sighing, she started to take another step.

And couldn't.

She couldn't go any farther. It was as if she'd reached the end of an invisible leash.

She went cold with disbelief. This was infuriating. He must have hypnotized her, but how? When? She couldn't remember him saying, *"You are getting sleepy,"* and she was pretty certain hypnosis didn't work that way, anyway. It was supposed to be a deep relaxation, not a do-things-against-your-will type of thing, regardless of how stage shows and movies portrayed it.

She wished she'd worn a watch, so she could have noticed any time discrepancy from when she'd gone into Raintree's office and when the fire alarm had sounded. She had to find out what time that had been, because she knew roughly what time sunset was. She'd been in his office for maybe half an hour…she thought. She couldn't be certain. Those disconcerting fantasies could have taken more time than she estimated.

Regardless of how he'd done it, he was controlling her movements. She knew it. When he said, "Stay with me," she'd stayed, even when faced with an inferno. When he said, "Don't go far," she had been able to go only so far and not a step farther.

She turned her head to look at him over her shoulder and found him standing more or less alone, evidently having finished answering whatever questions the other detective had asked. He was watching her, his expression grim. His lips moved. With all the background noise she couldn't hear what he was saying, but she read his lips plainly enough.

He said, "Come here."

Chapter 6

She went. She couldn't stop herself. Her scalp prickled, and chills ran over her, but she went, her feet moving automatically. Her eyes were wide with alarm. How was he doing this? Not that the "how" mattered; what mattered was *that* he was doing it. Being unable to control herself, to have *him* in control, could lead to some nasty situations.

She couldn't even ask for help, because no one would believe her. At best, people would think she was on drugs or was mentally unstable. All sympathy would be with him, because he'd just lost his casino, his livelihood; the last thing he needed was a nutcase accusing him of somehow controlling her movements. She could just see herself yelling, "Help! I'm walking, and I can't stop! He's making me do it!"

Yeah, right. That would work—*not*.

He gave her a grim, self-satisfied little smile as she neared, and that pissed her off. Being angry felt good; she didn't like being helpless in any way. Too street-savvy to telegraph her intentions, she kept her eyes wide, her expression alarmed, though how much of her face he could see through all the soot and grime was anyone's guess. She kept her right arm close to her side, her elbow bent a little, and tensed the muscles in her back and shoulder. When she was close, so close she could almost kiss him, she launched an uppercut toward his chin.

He never saw it coming, and her fist connected from below with a force that made his teeth snap together. Pain shot through her knuckles, but the satisfaction of punching him made it more than worthwhile. He staggered back half a step, then regained his balance with athletic grace, snaking out his hand to shackle her wrist with long fingers before she could hit him again. He used the grip to pull her against him.

"I deserved one punch," he said, holding her close as he bent his head to speak just loud enough for her to hear. "I won't take a second one."

"Let me go," she snapped. "And I don't mean just with your hand!"

"You've figured it out, then," he said coolly.

"I was a little slow on the uptake, but being shoved into the middle of a freaking, big-ass fire was distracting." She laid on the sarcasm as thickly as possible. "I don't know how you're doing it, or why—"

"The 'why,' at least, should be obvious."

"Then I must be oxygen-deprived from inhaling smoke—gee, I wonder whose fault that is—because it isn't obvious to me!"

"The little matter of your cheating me. Or did you think I'd forget about that in the excitement of watching my casino burn to the ground?"

"I haven't been— Wait a minute. Wait just a damn minute. You couldn't have hypnotized me while we were going down nineteen stories' worth of stairs, and if you did it while we were in your office, then that was before the fire even started. 'Splain that, Lucy!"

He grinned, his teeth flashing whitely in his soot-blackened face. "Am I supposed to say 'Oh, Ricky!'?"

"I don't care what you say. Just undo the voodoo, or the spell, or the hypnotism, or whatever it is you did. You can't hold me here like this."

"That's a ridiculous statement, when I obviously *am* holding you here like this."

Lorna thought steam might be coming out of

her ears. She'd been angry many times in her life—she'd even been enraged a couple of times—but this was the most *infuriated* she'd ever felt. Until tonight, she would have said that the three terms meant the same thing, but now she knew that being infuriated carried a rich measure of frustration with it. She was helpless, and she hated being helpless. Her entire life was built around the premise of not being helpless, not being a victim ever again.

"Let. Me. Go." Her teeth were clenched, her tone almost guttural. She was holding on to her self-control by a gossamer thread, but only because she knew screaming would get her exactly nowhere with him and would make *her* look like an idiot.

"Not yet. We still have a few issues to discuss." Completely indifferent to her temper, he lifted his head to look around at the scene of destruction. The stench of smoke permeated everything, and the flashing red and blue lights of many different emergency vehicles created a strobe effect that felt like a spike being pounded into her forehead. Hot spots still flared to crimson life in the smoldering ruins, until the vigilant firefighters targeted them with their hoses. A milling crowd pressed against the tape the police had strung up to cordon off the area.

She saw the same details he saw, and the flashing lights reminded her of a ball of flame…no, not of flame…something else. She gasped as her head gave a violent throb.

"Then discuss them, already," she snapped, putting her hand to her head in an instinctive gesture to contain the pain.

"Not here." He glanced down at her again. "Are you okay?"

"I have a splitting headache. I could go home and lie down, if you weren't being such a jerk."

He gave her a considering look. "But I *am* being a jerk, so sue me. Now be quiet and stay here like a good girl. I'll be busy for a while. When I'm finished, we'll go to my house and have that talk."

Lorna fell silent, and when he walked off she remained rooted to the spot. Damn him, she thought as furious tears welled in her eyes and streaked down her filthy cheeks. She raised her hands and wiped the tears away. At least he'd left her with the use of her hands. She couldn't walk and she couldn't talk, but she could dry her face, and if God was really kind to her, she could punch Raintree again the next time he got within punching distance.

Then she went cold, goose bumps rising on her entire body. The brief heat of anger died away, destroyed by a sudden, mind-numbing fear.

What was he?

* * *

A man and a woman who had been standing behind the police cordon, watching the massive fire, finally turned and began trudging toward their car. "Crap," the woman said glumly. Her name was Elyn Campbell, and she was the most powerful firemaster in the Ansara clan, except for the Dranir. Everything they knew about Dante Raintree, and everything she knew about fire—aided by some very powerful spells—had been added together to form a plan that should have resulted in the Raintree Dranir's death and instead had accomplished nothing of their mission.

"Yeah." Ruben McWilliams shook his head. All their careful planning, their calculations, up in smoke—literally. "Why didn't it work?"

"I don't know. It *should* have worked. He isn't that strong. No one is, not even a Dranir. It was overkill."

"Then evidently he's the strongest Dranir anyone's ever seen—either that or the luckiest."

"Or he quit sooner than we anticipated. Maybe he chickened out and ran for cover instead of trying to control it."

Ruben heaved a sigh. "Maybe. I didn't see when they brought him out, so maybe he'd been standing somewhere out of sight for a while before I finally spotted him. All that damn equipment was in the way."

She looked up at the starry sky. "So we have two possible scenarios. The first is that he chickened out and ran. The second, and unfortunately the most likely, is that he's stronger than we expected. Cael won't be happy."

Ruben sighed again and faced the inevitable. "I guess we've put it off long enough. We have to call in." He pulled his cell phone from his pocket, but the woman put her hand on his sleeve.

"Don't use your cell phone, it isn't encrypted. Wait until we get back to the hotel, and use a land line."

"Good idea." Anything that delayed placing this call to Cael Ansara was a good idea. Cael was his cousin on his mother's side, but kinship wouldn't cut any ice with the bastard—and he meant "bastard" both figuratively and literally. Maybe this secret alignment with Cael against the current Dranir, Judah, wasn't the smartest thing he'd ever done. Even though he'd agreed with Cael that the Ansara were now strong enough, after two hundred years of rebuilding, to take on the Raintree and destroy them, maybe he'd been wrong. Maybe Cael was wrong.

He knew Cael would automatically go for the first scenario, that Dante Raintree had chickened out and run instead of trying to contain the fire, and completely dismiss the possibility that Raintree was stronger than any of them had imagined.

But what if Raintree really *was* that powerful? The attempted coup Cael had planned would be a disaster, and the Ansara would be lucky to survive as a clan. It had taken two centuries to rebuild to their present strength after their last pitched battle with the Raintree.

Cael wouldn't be able to conceive of being wrong. If the plan failed—which it had—Cael would see only two possibilities: either Ruben and Elyn hadn't executed the plan correctly, or Raintree had revealed a cowardly streak. Ruben *knew* they hadn't made any mistakes. Everything had gone like clockwork—except for the outcome. Raintree was supposed to be consumed by a fire he couldn't control, a delicious irony, because firemasters all had a strange love/hate relationship with the force that danced to their tune. Instead, he had emerged unscathed. Filthy, sooty, maybe singed a little, but essentially unhurt.

A bullet to the head would have been more efficient, but Cael didn't want to do anything that would alert the Raintree clan, which an overt murder would certainly do. Everything had to be made to look accidental, which of course made guaranteeing the outcome more problematic. The royal family, the most powerful Raintrees, had to be taken out in such a way that no one suspected murder. A fire—they would think losing their Dranir in a fire was tragic and a bitter finale, but they would completely understand that he would fight to the end to save his casino and hotel, especially the hotel, with all the guests in residence there.

Cael, of course, wouldn't allow for the fact that setting up incidents that *didn't* point to the Ansara wasn't an exact science. Things could go wrong. Tonight, something had definitely gone wrong.

Dante Raintree was still alive. That was about as wrong as things could get.

The big assault on the Raintree homeplace, Sanctuary, was planned for the summer solstice, which was a week away. He and Elyn had a week to kill Dante Raintree—or Cael would kill *them*.

Chapter 7

Dante grimly walked back to where he'd left Lorna, reluctant to leave but knowing there was nothing else he could do here. Once the police were finished questioning him, his only thought had been to check on his employees to find out if there had been any fatalities. To his deep regret and fury, the answer to that last question was yes. One body had already been pulled from the smoldering ruins of the casino, and the cops were working with the crowd to establish if there were any missing friends or relatives, which would take time. There might not be a final count for a couple of days.

He'd found Al Rayburn, hoarse and coughing

from smoke inhalation but refusing to go to a hospital, instead helping to keep order among the evacuated guests. The hotel staff was doing an admirable job. The hotel itself had suffered comparatively little damage, and most of that was to the lobby area that connected the hotel and casino, where Dante had made his stand. Everyone in the hotel, guests and staff, had safely evacuated. There were some minor injuries, sprained ankles and the like, but nothing major. There was smoke damage, of course, and the entire hotel would have to be cleaned to remove the stench. The good news, what there was of it, was that the parking deck hadn't been damaged, and the hotel had no structural damage. He could probably re-open the hotel within two weeks. The question was: why would anyone want to stay there without the casino?

The casino was a complete loss. About twenty vehicles in the parking lot outside the casino entrance had been damaged, and the parking lot itself was a mess right now. Twenty or thirty people had burns of varying degrees, and as many again were suffering from smoke inhalation; all of them had been transported to local hospitals.

The media had descended en masse, of course, their constant shouts and interruptions and requests/demands for interviews interfering with his attempts to organize his employees, arrange other lodging for his hotel guests, and arrange with Al for the guests to retrieve their belongings and at the same time secure the hotel from thieves posing as guests. He had his insurance provider to deal with. He had to call Gideon and Mercy, to let them know about the fire and that he was all right, before they saw all this on the news. They were both in the Eastern Time Zone, meaning he'd better get in touch with them damn soon.

Finally he'd accepted that there was little more he could do tonight; his staff was excellent, and they had matters well in hand, plus he could always be reached by phone. He might as well go home and take a much-needed shower.

And that left the problem of Lorna.

Tonight was a night of firsts. Before tonight, he'd never used mind compulsion, never known he could. He had no idea what the parameters were. At first he'd thought his own sense of urgency had provided the impetus, but even after the evacuation was over, he'd been able to control Lorna just with the words and a nudge from his mind, so adrenaline wasn't the catalyst. He had stepped into new territory, and he had to tread lightly because this particular power could be easily abused. Hell, he'd already abused it, hadn't he? Lorna would definitely say yes to that—when he let her speak.

Tonight was also the first time he'd brutally

overwhelmed someone else's mind and literally stolen all their available power. In the aftermath, she'd been dazed, lethargic, unable to remember even her name, all symptoms attributable to emotional shock. How extensive the amnesia was, and how temporary, was something that remained to be seen. She'd begun recovering fairly soon, but she still didn't remember vast portions of the experience—unless she'd recovered her memory in his absence, in which case he should probably find some body armor before he released her from the compulsion.

Was she Ansara? That was the burning question that had to be answered—and soon.

His thinking went both ways. Part of him said, no, she couldn't possibly be, or he wouldn't have been able to overpower her mind so easily, nor would she be so susceptible to mind compulsion. An Ansara, trained from birth to manage and control her unusual abilities, just as the Raintree were, would have automatically resisted mind compulsion. The power was rare, so rare that he'd never met anyone capable of exercising it, though the family history said that an aunt six generations back had been adept at it. Rare or not, because the power existed at all, he and every other Raintree had been taught how to construct mental shields. The Ansara basically mirrored the Raintree in their gifts, so undoubtedly they, too, taught their people how to shield, which meant that the completely unshielded Lorna could not be Ansara.

Unless…

Unless she was so gifted at shielding that he couldn't detect it. Unless she was merely pretending to be controlled by mind compulsion. He'd spoken his will aloud, so she knew what he wanted. If she also had the gift of controlling fire, she could have been bolstering the blaze, resurrecting the flames every time he managed to beat them down. No. He rejected that idea. If she'd been the one feeding the fire, he would have been able to extinguish it completely after he'd commandeered her power. Someone else must have been feeding the fire, but she could have been distracting him, deflecting some of his power.

Was she or wasn't she? He would know soon. If she wasn't…then he'd played some real hardball with a woman who might not be an innocent but was still far from being an enemy. He didn't know that he would have done anything differently, though. When he'd overwhelmed her mind, it had been an act of desperation, and he hadn't had the luxury of time to explain things to her. He might have to make amends, but he wasn't sorry he'd done it. He was just glad she'd been there, glad she was gifted and had a pool of mental energy for him to tap.

He rounded a fire engine, where the crew was laying out their hoses in preparation for recoiling them, and stepped up on a curb. Now he could see her. So far as he could tell, she was standing in the exact spot in which he'd left her, which at least was off to the side, so she wasn't in the way of any of the firefighters. She was filthy, her hair matted from the unhappy combination of smoke, soot and water, her posture shouting exhaustion. She still clutched a blanket around her, and she was literally swaying where she stood. He felt a quick spurt of impatience, mingled with sympathy. Why hadn't she sat down? He hadn't prevented her from doing that.

Looking at her, he gave a mental wince on behalf of his car seats, then immediately shrugged, because he was just as filthy. What did it matter, anyway? The leather could be cleaned.

When she saw him, pure temper flashed in her eyes, dispelling the fatigue. If he'd expected her to be cowed, he would have been disappointed. As it was, a little tinge of anticipation shot through him. Even after all she'd been through, she was still standing up for herself. Remembering the vast pool of power he'd found when he tapped her mind, he wondered if even she knew how strong she really was.

"Come with me," he said, and, obediently, she followed.

There was nothing obedient about the way she grabbed his arm, though, pulling him around. She glared furiously up at him, indicating her mouth with a brief, impatient gesture. She wanted to talk; she probably had a lot of things memorized to say.

Dante started to release the compulsion, then stopped and grinned. "I think I'll enjoy the quiet for a little longer," he said, knowing that would really twist her drawers in a knot. "There's nothing you need to say that can't wait until we're alone."

Al had arranged for one of his security people to fetch Dante's car from the parking deck, where he had a reserved slot next to a private elevator. He'd been discreet about it, because some of the guests, the ones without identification, weren't being allowed to take their vehicles from the deck. They were already sorting out that security problem for those guests who felt they absolutely had to have a car tonight, even though Dante was providing shuttles to take everyone to the various hotels where his people had found them lodging. He was doing everything possible to take care of his guests, but he knew there could still be a lot of resentment that formed over details like him getting his car when they couldn't.

The phantom-black Lotus Exige was idling, parking lights on, at the end of the huge casino parking lot, concealed from most of the crowd of onlookers by the huge knot of emergency vehicles with their flashing lights. Dante led Lorna along the edge of the lot; as they neared the car, the driver's door opened and one of the security men got out. "Here you go, Mr. Raintree."

"Thanks, Jose." Dante opened the passenger door. Lorna directed a lethal glare at him as she climbed into the car and somehow managed to dig an elbow into his ribs. He concealed a wince, then closed the door with a firm click and went around to the driver's side.

The Lotus was low-slung and not all that comfortable for his muscular six-two frame, but he loved driving it when he was in the mood for something with attitude. When he wanted more comfort, he drove his Jag. Tonight he would have liked to drive out into the desolate countryside and put the hammer down, to ease his anger and sharp edge of sorrow with sheer speed and aggression. The Lotus could go from zero to a hundred in eleven seconds, which was a rush. He needed to go a hundred miles an hour right now, needed to push the high-performance little machine to its limit.

Instead he drove calmly and deliberately, aware that he couldn't let go of the tight leash he was holding on his temper. The fact that it was night helped, but the date was too close to the summer solstice for him to take any chances. Hell—could *he* have started the accursed fire? Was *he* responsible for the loss of at least one life?

The fire marshal said preliminary interviews indicated that it had started in the back, where the circuit breakers were, but the scene was still too hot for the investigators to get in there to check. If the fire had started from an electrical problem, then he had nothing to do with it, but he brooded over the possibility that the fire would turn out to have been started by something completely different. His control had wavered when he'd first seen Lorna, with the last rays of the setting sun turning her hair to rich fire. He'd lit the candles without even thinking about them; had he lit anything else?

No, he hadn't done it. He was sure of that. If he'd been the cause, things would have been bursting into flame all over the hotel and casino, rather than in one distant spot. He'd contained his power, brought it under control. The casino fire had been caused by something else; the timing was just coincidence.

Almost half an hour had lapsed before he opened his gate with a remote control and guided the Lotus up a twisting, curving drive to his tri-level house tucked into an eastern-facing fold of the Sierra Nevadas. Another button on the remote raised his garage door, and he put the Lotus in its slot like an astronaut docking a shuttle with the Space Station, then closed the garage door behind him. The silver Jag gleamed in its place beside the Lotus.

"Come on," he told Lorna, and she got out of the car. She stared straight ahead as he stepped aside to allow her to precede him into his gleaming kitchen. He punched his code into the security system to stop its warning beep, then paused. He briefly considered taking her back to town after he'd finished talking to her, then discarded that idea. He was tired. She could stay here, and if he had to—as he undoubtedly would—he would use a compulsion to keep her here and out of trouble. If she didn't like it, tough; the last couple of hours had been a bitch, and he didn't feel like making the drive.

With that in mind, he reset the alarm and turned to her. She was standing with her back to him, not four feet away, her shoulders stiff and, judging by the angle of her head, her chin up.

Regretting the imminent loss of silence, he said, "Okay, you can talk now."

She whirled to face him, and he braced himself for a flood of invective as her fists clenched at her sides.

"Bathroom!" she bellowed at him.

Chapter 8

The change in his expression would have been comical if Lorna had been in any mood to appreciate humor. His eyes rounded with comprehension, and he rapidly pointed to a short hallway. "First door on the right."

She took one frantic step, and then froze. Damn it, he was still holding her! The searing look she gave him should have accomplished what the casino fire hadn't, namely singe every hair from his head. "Don't go far," he snapped, realizing he hadn't amended the compulsion.

Lorna ran. She slammed the bathroom door but didn't take time to lock it. She barely made it in time, and the sense of relief was so acute she shook with involuntary shudders. A Tom Hanks scene from *A League of Their Own* ran through her mind, and she bit her lip to keep from groaning aloud.

Then she just sat there, eyes closed, trying to calm her jangled nerves. He'd brought her to his *home!* What did he intend to do? Whatever he was, however, he was controlling her, she was helpless to break free. The entire time he'd been gone, she had been willing herself over and over to take a single step, to speak a word—and she couldn't. She was scared half out of her mind, traumatized out of the other half, and on top of it all, she was so angry she thought she might have a screaming, out-of-control, foot-stomping temper tantrum just to relieve the pressure.

Opening her eyes, she started to flush, but she heard his voice and went still, straining to hear what he was saying. Was someone else here? Just as she began to relax just a fraction, she realized he was on the phone.

"Sorry to wake you." He paused briefly, then said, "There was a fire at the casino. Could be worse, but it's bad enough. I didn't want you to see it on the morning news and wonder. Call Mercy in a couple of hours and tell her I'm all right. I've got a feeling I'm going to have my hands full for the next few days."

Another pause. "Thanks, but no. You've got no business getting on an airplane this week, and everything here is fine. I just wanted to call you before I got so tied up in red tape I couldn't get to a phone."

The conversation continued for a minute, and he kept reassuring whoever was on the other end that no, he didn't need help; everything was fine—well, not fine, but under control. There had been at least one fatality. The casino was a total loss, but the hotel had suffered only minor damage.

He ended the call, and a moment later Lorna heard a savage, muttered curse, then a thud, as if he'd punched the wall.

He didn't seem like the wall-punching type, she thought. Then again, she didn't know him. He might be a serial wall-puncher. Or maybe he'd fainted or something, and the thud had been his body hitting the floor.

She liked that idea. She would seize the chance to kick him while he was down. Literally.

The only way to see if he was lying there unconscious was to leave the bathroom. Reluctantly, she flushed, then went to the vanity to wash her hands—a vanity with a dark, golden-brown granite top and gold fixtures. When she reached out to turn on the water, the contrast between the richness of the vanity and her absolutely filthy, blacksooted hand made her inwardly cringe as she lifted her head.

A grimy nightmare loomed in the mirror in front of her. Her hair was matted to her head with soot and water, and stank of smoke. Her face was so black only her eyes had any real definition, and they were bloodshot. With her red eyes, she looked like some demon from hell.

She shuddered, remembering how close the flames had gotten. Given that, she couldn't imagine how she had any hair left on her head at all, so she shouldn't complain about it being matted. Shampoo—a lot of it—would take care of that. The soot would scrub off. Her clothes were ruined, but she had others. She was alive and unharmed, and she didn't know how.

As she soaped her grimy hands, rinsed, then soaped again, she tried to reconstruct an exact sequence of events. Her headache, which had subsided, roared back so fiercely she had to brace her soapy hands on the edge of the bowl.

Thoughts whirled, trying to connect in a coherent sequence, but then the segments would whirl out of touch again.

—she should have been burned—

—hair singed off—

—bubble—

—no smoke—

—agony—

Whimpering from the pain in her head, she sank to her knees.

Raintree cursing.

Something about that reminded her of something. Of being held in front of him, his arms locked around her, while his curses rang out over her head and his…his—

The memory was gone, eluding her grasp. Pain made her vision swim, and she stared at the soap bubbles on her hands, trying to summon the energy to stand. Was she having a stroke? The pain was so intense, burning, and it filled her head until she thought her skull might explode from the pressure.

Soap bubbles.

The shimmery bubbles…something about them reminded her…there had been something around her….

A *shimmering bubble*. The memory burst into her aching brain, so clear it brought tears to her eyes. She'd *seen* it, surrounding them, holding the heat and smoke at bay.

Her head had felt as if it really were exploding then. There had been an impact so huge she couldn't compare it to anything in her experience, but she imagined the sensation was the same as if she'd been run over by a train—or struck by a meteor. It was as if all the cellular walls in her brain had dissolved, as if everything she had been, was, and would be, had been sucked out, taken over and used. She'd been helpless, as completely helpless as a newborn, to resist the pain or the man who had ruthlessly taken everything.

With a crash, everything fell back into place, as if that memory had been the one piece she needed to put the puzzle together.

She remembered it all: every moment of unspeakable terror, her inability to act, the way he had used her.

Everything.

"You've had enough time," he called from the kitchen. "I heard you flush. Come here, Lorna."

Like a puppet, she got to her feet and walked out of the bathroom, soap still clinging to her hands and her temper flaring. He looked grim, standing there waiting for her. With every unwilling step she took, her temper soared into another level of the stratosphere.

"You *jerk!*" she shouted, and kicked his ankle as she walked by. She could go only a couple of steps past him before that invisible wall stopped her, so she whirled around and stalked past him again. "You *ass!*" She threw an elbow into his ribs.

She must not have hurt him very much because he looked more astonished than pained. That infuriated her even more, and when the wall forced her to turn around yet again, she reached a whole new level of temper as she began marching back and forth within the confines of his will.

"You made me go into *fire*—" A snake-fast pinch at his waist.

"I'm *terrified* of fire, but did you *care?*" Another kick, this one sideways into his knee.

"Oh, no, I had to *stand there* while you did your mumbo jumbo—" On that pass, she leveled a punch at his solar plexus.

"Then you *brain-raped* me, you jerk, you gorilla, you freakin' *witch doctor*—" On the return trip, she went for a kidney punch.

"Then, to top it all off, the whole time you were *grinding your hard-on against my butt!*" She was so incensed that she shrieked that last bit at him, and this time put everything she had into a punch straight to his chin.

He blocked it with a swift movement of his forearm, so she stomped on his foot instead.

"Ouch!" he yelped, but the jerk was *laughing*, damn him, and in another of his lightning moves, he captured her in his arms, pulling her solidly against him. She opened her mouth to screech at him, and he bent his head and kissed her.

In contrast to the strong-arm tactics he'd used against her all night, the kiss was soft and feather-light, almost sweet. "I'm sorry," he murmured, and kissed her again. He stank as much as she did, maybe even more, but the body beneath his ruined clothing was rock solid with muscle and very warm in the air-conditioned coolness of the house. "I know it hurt… I didn't have time to explain—" Between phrases, he kept on kissing her, each successive touch of his lips becoming a little deeper, lingering a little longer.

Shock held her still: shock that he would be kissing her; shock that she would *let* him kiss her, after all the antagonism between them; after he'd done everything he'd done to her; after she'd subjected him to that battery of drive-by attacks. He wasn't forcing her to let him kiss her; this was nothing like wanting to walk and not being able to. Her hands were on his muscled chest, but she wasn't making any effort to push him away, not even a mental one.

His mouth slid to the soft hollow beneath her ear, deposited a gentle bite on the site of her neck. "I'd much rather have been grinding my hard-on against your front," he said, and went back to her mouth for a kiss that had nothing light or sweet about it. His tongue swept in, acquainting him with her taste, while his right hand went down to her bottom, slid caressingly over the curves, then pressed her hips forward to meet his.

He was doing exactly what he'd said he would much rather have been doing.

Lorna didn't trust passion. From what she had seen, passion was selfish and self-centered. She wasn't immune to it, but she didn't trust it—didn't trust men, who in her experience would tell lies just to get laid. She didn't trust anyone else to care about her, to look out for her interests. She opened herself to passion slowly, warily, if at all.

If she hadn't been so tired, so stressed, so traumatized, she would have had complete control of herself, but she'd been off balance from the minute his chief of security had escorted her into his office. She was off balance now, as dizzy as if the kitchen were rotating around her, as if the floor had slanted beneath her feet. In contrast, he was solid and so very warm, his arms stronger than any that had ever held her before, and her body responded to him as if nothing else existed beyond the simple pleasure of the moment. Being held against him felt good. His incredible body heat felt good. The thick length of his erection, pushing against her lower belly, felt good—so good that she had gone on tiptoe to better accommodate it, and she didn't remember doing so.

Belatedly alarmed by the no-show of her usual caution, she pulled her mouth from his and pushed against his chest. "This is stupid," she muttered.

"Brainless," he agreed, his breath coming a little fast. He was slow to release her, so she pushed again, and, reluctantly, he let his arms drop.

He didn't step back, so she did, staring around her at the kitchen so she wouldn't have to look at him. As kitchens went, it was nice, she supposed. She didn't like cooking, so in the general scheme of things, kitchens were pretty much wasted on her.

"You kidnapped me," she charged, scowling at him.

He considered that, then gave a brief nod. "I did."

For some reason his agreement annoyed her more than if he'd argued with her assessment. "If you're going to charge me with cheating, then do it," she snapped. "You can't prove a thing, and we both know it, so the sooner you make a fool of yourself, the better, as far as I'm concerned, because then I can leave and not see you—"

"I'm not making any charges against you," he interrupted. "You're right. I can't prove anything."

His sudden admission stumped her. "Then why drag me all the way up here?"

"I said I can't prove you did it. That doesn't mean you're innocent." He gave her a narrow, assessing look. "In fact, you're guilty as hell. Using your paranormal gifts in a game of chance is cheating, pure and simple."

"I don't have—" Automatically, she started to

deny that she was psychic, but he raised a hand to cut her off.

"That's why I did the 'brain-rape,' as you called it. I needed an extra reserve of power to hold off the fire, and I knew you were gifted—but I was surprised at *how* gifted. You can't tell me you didn't know. There was too much power there for you to pass yourself off as just being lucky."

Lorna hardly knew how to react. His cool acknowledgment of what he'd done to her raised her hackles all over again, but the charge that she was "gifted" made her so uneasy that she was already shaking her head before he finished speaking. "Numbers," she blurted. "I'm good with numbers."

"Bull."

"That's all it is! I don't tell fortunes or read tea leaves or anything like that! I didn't know 9/11 was going to happen—"

But the flight numbers of the downed flights had haunted her for days before the attack. If she tried to dial a phone number, the numbers she dialed were those flight numbers—in the order in which the planes had crashed.

That particular memory surfaced like a salmon leaping out of the water, and a chill shook her. She hadn't thought of the flight numbers since then. She had buried the memory deep, where it couldn't cause trouble.

"Go away," she whispered to the memory.

"I'm not going anywhere," he said. "And neither are you. At least, not right away." He sighed and gave her a regretful look. "Take off your clothes."

Chapter 9

"I will not!" Lorna yelped, backing as far away from him as she could get, which of course wasn't far.

"So will I, probably," he replied ironically, moving closer, looming over her. "Can't be helped. Look, I'm not going to assault you. Just take off your clothes and get it over with."

She retreated as he advanced, clutching at her blouse as if she were an outraged Victorian virgin and looking around for a weapon, any weapon. This was a kitchen, damn it; it was supposed to have knives sitting in a fancy block on the fancy countertop. Instead, there was nothing but a vast expanse of polished granite.

He took a deep breath, then heaved it out as if he were bored. "I can make you do it without even touching you. You know that, and I know that, so why do this the hard way?"

He was right, she thought impotently. Whatever it was that his mind did to her mind, he could make her do anything he wanted. "This isn't fair!" she shouted at him, curling her hands into fists. "How are you *doing* this to me?"

"I'm a freakin' witch doctor, remember?"

"Don't forget the rest of it! Jerk! Ass—"

"I know, I know. Now take off your clothes."

She shook her head, matted hair flying. Bitterly, she expected him to take control of her mind, but he didn't. He just inexorably advanced as she retreated, backing down the hallway past the powder room she'd used, through what she assumed was a very stylish den, though she didn't dare take her gaze from him long enough to look around.

He was herding her, she realized, as if she were a sheep, and she had no choice, but to do anything other than be herded. His bloodshot green eyes glittered in his grimy face, making him look completely uncivilized. Her heartbeat skittered wildly. Was he some sort of mad serial killer who left pieces of dismembered bodies scattered all over Nevada? A modern-day Rasputin? An escapee from some mental institution? He certainly didn't look or act like the millionaire owner of a top-notch casino/hotel. He acted like some sort of—of warlord, master of all he surveyed.

She backed into a door frame, briefly staggered off balance, then brought herself up short as she realized he'd maneuvered her into another bathroom, this one a full bath, and far more opulent than the half bath off the kitchen. No lights were on, but the illumination coming in the open door revealed their reflections in the gleaming mirror on her left.

He reached in and flipped on the lights, so bright and white that she lifted a hand to shield her eyes. "Now," he said, "no more stalling. Take off your clothes yourself, or we'll do this the hard way."

Lorna looked around. She was cornered. "Go to hell," she said, and did what cornered animals always do: she attacked.

For a short while he merely blocked her punches, deflected her kicks, avoided her bites, and the ease with which he did so made her that much angrier. She lost one shoe in the battle, the cheap sandal sailing across the room to clatter into the huge sunken tub. Then she felt a sudden wave of impatience emanating from him, and in three seconds flat he had her bent over the vanity with her hands pinned behind her.

He crowded in close, using his powerful legs to control her kicks, and gripped the neckline of her top. Three hard yanks brought the sound of several threads giving way, but the seams held. He cursed and yanked harder, and the left-side seam surrendered. Ruthlessly he tore at the garment until it was in rags, hanging from her right wrist. Her bra fastened in back, easy prey to the quick pinch of his fingers that released the hooks.

She squirmed like an eel, screaming until she was hoarse. He completely ignored everything she said, every insult and plea she hurled at him, silently and grimly concentrating on stripping her. She alternated between fury and sobs of panic as he opened the fastening of her pants, lowered the zipper, but stopped before pushing her pants and underwear down over her hips.

She went limp, sobbing, her face pressed against the cold stone of the vanity. He stopped pulling at her clothes, and instead the heat of his hand moved over her neck, lifting her matted hair aside for a moment, then tracing over her shoulders. He shifted his grip on her hands, instead pulling them up and over her head before resuming what felt like an inch-by-inch search of her skin. The sides of her breasts, her ribs, the indentation of her waist, the flare of her hips—he examined all of that, even pushing her pants lower to scrutinize the bottom curves of her buttocks. Mortified, she squirmed and sobbed, but he was inexorable.

Then he sighed and said, "I owe you another apology."

He released his grip on her hands and stepped back, freeing her from the pressure of his body. On his way out he said, "I'll bring you some clothes. Think about taking a shower, get your breath back and we'll talk afterward." He paused, added, "Don't leave this room," then quietly closed the door.

Sobbing, she slid from the vanity to the floor and curled in a vanquished heap. At first all she could do was cry and shake. After a while her temper resurrected itself and flashed over in a wordless shriek. She wept some more. Finally she sat up, wiped her face with the shreds of her blouse, yelled, "You bastard!" at the door, and felt marginally better for the invective.

Her eyes were swollen and her nose was clogged, but she felt calm enough to stand, though that wasn't easy with her pants around her knees. The indignity made her flush with humiliation, but there was no point in pulling them up. Instead she stripped completely naked and stood there in rare indecision.

The suggestion to take a shower, she discovered, had been just that: a suggestion. If she didn't want to, she didn't have to. She could take a long soak in the sunken tub, if she wished. She didn't have to bathe at all, though that was an option she immediately discarded.

Getting in the tub wouldn't be practical, because she would end up sitting in dirty water. A long—very long—hot shower was the only way to get clean.

The shower didn't have a door. The entrance was a curved wall of stone that led past a built-in shelf, stacked with thick, copper-colored towels, to three steps down into a five-foot-square stall with multiple showerheads. The controls were within easy reach, and when she turned the handle, water spurted out of three walls and from overhead. She waited until she felt the heat of the steam rising to her face, then stepped into the deluge.

Concentrating on getting clean, and nothing else, gave her nerves a much-needed respite. The hot water streaming over her body was a soothing, pulsating massage. She shampooed and rinsed, then did it again, and yet again, before her hair felt clean and untangled. She lathered and scrubbed with the fragrant bath gel, and found it didn't remove even half the soot and grime. A second scrubbing produced results that weren't much better, so she switched back to the shampoo; it had worked on her hair, so it should work on her skin.

Finally she realized that she'd been in the shower so long that her fingertips had wrinkled and the hot water should have long since been used up, though it wasn't—but enough was enough. She was waterlogged. Regretfully, she turned off the water, and the pulsating streams disappeared so suddenly that it was as if they'd been sucked back into the showerheads. Only the sounds of the vent fan overhead and the draining water came to her ears.

She hadn't turned on the vent fan. Unless it came on automatically when the humidity level reached a certain point, he'd come back into the bathroom.

Hurriedly, she went up the three steps, grabbed one of the fluffy towels and wrapped it around herself, then got another one and twisted it into a turban over her dripping hair. Following the curving wall, she moved until she could see into the main part of the bathroom. The mirrored wall behind the double sinks threw her reflection back at her, but hers was the only reflection. She was alone—now. The thick terry-cloth robe folded over the vanity stool told her that he *had* been there.

Lorna stared at the mirror. She looked pale, even to herself. The skin across her cheekbones was drawn tight, giving her a stark, shocked expression.

That was okay. She *felt* stark and shocked.

He'd said not to leave the bathroom. She was so soul-weary that she didn't even try, so she didn't know if that had been another suggestion or one

of his weird mental orders that she couldn't dis-
obey. At this point it didn't matter whether it was
a suggestion or command. She was content to
simply stay there, where there was nothing more
complicated to do than dry her hair.

Rummaging in the drawers of the vanity, she
found scented lotion, as well as a hair dryer and
brush, which was all she needed right now. The
shampoo had made her skin feel tight, so she
rubbed in the lotion everywhere she could reach,
then began the task of drying her hair.

Her motions with the brush became slower,
then slower still. Exhaustion made her arms trem-
ble. She was lucky that her hair was mostly
straight, and had good body, because any attempt
at styling it was beyond her. She just wanted her
hair to be dry before she collapsed, that was all.

With that chore accomplished, she put on the
robe, which was evidently his; the sleeves fell
several inches past the tips of her fingers and the
hem almost reached the floor. Funny, she thought
fuzzily, he didn't seem like the robe-wearing type.

Then she waited, swaying on her feet, her bare
toes clenching on the plush rug. She could have at
least opened the door, but she wasn't in any rush to
face him, or to find out that even with the door
open, she was imprisoned in this room. Time enough
for that. Time enough to engage the enemy again.

They would talk, he'd said. She didn't want to talk to him. She had nothing to say to him that didn't involve a lot of four-letter words. All she wanted was to go…well, not *home*, exactly, because she didn't have a home in that sense. She wanted to go back to where she was staying, to where her clothes were. That was close enough to home for her. For now, she just wanted to sleep in the bed she was accustomed to.

Without warning, the door opened and he stood there, tall and broad-shouldered, as vital as if the night hadn't been long and traumatic. He'd showered, too; his longish black hair, still damp, was brushed straight back to reveal every strong, faintly exotic line of his face. He'd shaved, too; his face had that freshly scraped look.

He was wearing a pair of very soft-looking pajama pants…and nothing else. Not even a smile.

His keen eyes searched her face, noting the white look of utter exhaustion. "We'll talk in the morning. I doubt you could form a coherent sentence right now. Come on, I'll show you where your room is."

She shrank back, and he looked at her with an unreadable expression. "*Your* room," he emphasized. "Not mine. I didn't make that a command, but I will if necessary. I don't think you'd be comfortable sleeping in the bathroom."

She was awake enough to retort, "You'll have to make it a command, otherwise I can't leave the bathroom, anyway."

She had decided that his command not to leave the bathroom had been meant to short-circuit her own will, and by his flash of irritation, she saw she'd been right.

"Come with me," he said curtly, a command that released her from the bathroom but sentenced her to follow him like a duckling.

He led her to a spacious bedroom with seven-foot windows that revealed the sparkling neon colors of Reno. "The private bath is through there," he said, indicating a door. "You're safe. I won't bother you. I won't hurt you. Don't leave this room." With that, he closed the door behind him and left her standing in the dimly lit bedroom.

He *would* remember to tack on that last sentence, damn him—not that she felt capable of making a run for it. Right now her capability was limited to climbing into the king-size bed, still wearing the oversize robe. She curled under the sheet and duvet, but still felt too exposed, so she pulled the sheet over her head and slept.

Chapter 10

Monday

"Are you okay?"

Lorna woke, as always, to a lingering sense of dread and fear. It wasn't the words that alarmed her, though, since she immediately recognized the voice. They were, however, far from welcome. Regardless of where she was, the dread was always there, within her, so much a part of her that it was as if it had been beaten into her very bones.

She couldn't see him, because the sheet was still over her head. She seldom moved in her sleep, so she was still in such a tight curl that the oversize robe hadn't been dislodged or even come untied.

"Are you okay?" he repeated, more insistently.

"Peachy keen," she growled, wishing he would just go away again.

"You were making a noise."

"I was snoring," she said flatly, keeping a tight grip on the sheet in case he tried to pull it down— like she could stop him if he really wanted to. She had learned the futility of that in the humiliating struggle last night.

He snorted. "Yeah, right." He paused. "How do you like your coffee?"

"I don't. I'm a tea drinker."

Silence greeted that for a moment; then he sighed. "I'll see what I can do. How do you drink your tea?"

"With friends."

She heard what sounded remarkably like a growl, then the bedroom door closed with more force than necessary. Had she sounded ungrateful? *Good!* After everything he'd done, if he thought the offer of coffee or tea would make up for it, he was so far off base he wasn't even in the ballpark.

Truth to tell, she wasn't much of a tea drinker, either. For most of her life she'd been able to afford only what was free, which meant she drank a lot of water. In the last few years she'd had the occasional cup of coffee or hot tea, to warm up in very cold weather, but she didn't really care for either of them.

She didn't want to get up. She didn't want to have that talk he seemed bent on, though what he thought they had to talk about, she couldn't imagine. He'd treated her horribly last night, and though he'd evidently realized he was wrong, he didn't seem inclined to go out of his way to make amends. He hadn't, for instance, taken her home last night. He'd imprisoned her in this room. He hadn't even fed the prisoner!

The empty ache in her stomach told her that she had to get out of bed if she wanted food. Getting out of bed didn't guarantee she would get fed, of course, but staying in bed certainly guaranteed she wouldn't. Reluctantly, she flipped the sheet back, and the first thing she saw was Dante Raintree, standing just inside the door. The bully hadn't left at all; he'd just pretended to.

He lifted one eyebrow in a silent, sardonic question.

Annoyed, she narrowed her eyes at him. "That's inhuman."

"What is?"

"Lifting just one eyebrow. Real people can't do that. Just demons."

"*I* can do it."

"Which proves my point."

He grinned—which annoyed her even more, because she didn't want to amuse him. "If you want to get up, this demon has washed your clothes—"

"What you didn't shred," she interjected sourly, to hide her alarm. Had he emptied her pockets first? She didn't ask, because if he hadn't, maybe her money and license were still there.

"—and loaned you one of his demon shirts. You'll probably have to throw your pants away, because the stains won't come out, but at least they're clean. They'll do for now. Your choices for breakfast are cereal and fruit, or a bagel and cream cheese. When you get dressed, come to the kitchen. We'll eat in there." He left then—really left, because she watched him go.

He was assuming she would share a meal with him. Unfortunately, he was right. She was starving, and if the only way she could get some food was to sit anywhere in his vicinity, then she would sit there. One of the first lessons she'd learned about life was that emotions didn't carry much weight when survival sat on the other end of the scale.

Slowly she sat up, feeling aches and twinges in every muscle. Her newly washed, stained-beyond-redemption pants lay across the foot of the bed, as well as her underwear and a white shirt made out of some limp, slinky material. She grabbed for the pants and dug her hand into each pocket, and her heart sank. Not only was her money gone, but so was her license. He either had them, or they had fallen out in the wash, which meant she had to find the laundry room in this place and search the washer and dryer. Maybe he had someone working for him who did the laundry; maybe that person had taken her money and ID.

She got out of bed and hobbled to the bathroom. After taking care of her most urgent business, she looked in the drawers of the vanity, hoping he was a good host—even if he was a lousy person—and had stocked the bathroom with emergency supplies. She desperately needed a toothbrush.

He was a good host. She found everything she needed: a supply of toothbrushes still in their sealed plastic cases, toothpaste, mouthwash, the same scented lotion she'd used the night before, a small sewing kit, even new hairbrushes and disposable razors.

The toothbrush manufacturer had evidently not intended for anyone without a knife or scissors to be able to use their product. After struggling to tear the plastic case apart, first with her fingers and then with her teeth, she got the tiny pair of scissors from the sewing kit and laboriously stabbed, sawed and hacked until she had freed the incarcerated toothbrush. She regarded the scissors thoughtfully, then laid them on the vanity top. They were too small to be of much use, but…

After brushing her teeth and washing her face, she dragged a brush through her hair. Good enough. Even if she'd had her skimpy supply of makeup with her, she wouldn't have put any on for Raintree's benefit.

Going back into the bedroom, she locked the door just in case he decided to waltz in again, then removed the robe and began dressing. The precaution was useless, she thought bitterly, because if he wanted in, all he had to do was order her to unlock the door and she would do what he said, whether she wanted to or not. She *hated* that, and she hated *him*.

She didn't want to put on his shirt. She picked it up and turned it so she could see the tag. She didn't recognize the brand name, but that wasn't what she was looking for, anyway. The tag with the care instructions read 100% Silk—Dry-clean Only.

Maybe she could smear some jelly on the shirt. Accidentally, of course.

She started to slip her arms into the sleeves, then paused, remembering how he'd phrased his last statement: *When you're dressed, come to the kitchen.* Once she was dressed, she probably wouldn't have a choice about going to the kitchen, so anything she wanted to do, she should do before putting on that shirt.

She dropped the shirt back on the bed and retrieved the tiny scissors from the bathroom, slipping them into her right pocket. Then she systematically searched both the bathroom and bedroom, looking for anything she might use as a weapon or to help her somehow escape. If she saw any opening, however small, she had to be prepared to take it.

One big obstacle was that she didn't have any shoes. She doubted the ones she'd been wearing could be saved, but at least they would protect her feet. Raintree hadn't brought them to the bedroom, but they might still be in the bathroom she'd used last night. She didn't want to run barefoot through the countryside, though she would if she had to. How far would she have to run before she was free? How far out did Raintree's sphere of influence reach? There had to be a distance at which his mind tricks wouldn't work—didn't there? Did she have to hear him speak the command, or could he just *think* it at her?

Uneasily, she hoped he had somehow simply hypnotized her, because otherwise she was so deep in *The Twilight Zone* doo-doo she might never get the weird crap off her shoes.

Other than the scissors, neither the bath nor the bedroom supplied anything usable. There were no pistols in the built-in drawers, no stray hammer she

could use to bash him in the head, not even any
extra clothes in the huge closet that she could have
used to suffocate him. Regretfully, with no other
option left, she finally put on the silk shirt. As she
was rolling up the too-long sleeves, she wondered
when the command stuff would kick in. The slip-
pery material didn't roll up very well, so she redid
the sleeves several times before she gave up and let
the rolls droop over her wrists. Even then, she
didn't feel an irresistible urge to go to the kitchen.

She was on her own. He hadn't put the command mojo on her.

Tremendously annoyed that, under her own free
will, she was doing what he'd told her to do anyway, she unlocked the bedroom door and stepped
out into the hallway.

Two sets of stairs opened before her, the one on
the right going up to the next floor and leading to
what appeared to be a balcony. The set on the left
went down, widening to a graceful fan at the
bottom. She frowned, not remembering any stairs
from the night before. Had she been that out of it?
She definitely remembered arriving at the house,
remembered noticing that it had three separate
levels, so of course there were stairs—she just
didn't remember them. Having this kind of hole
in her memory was frightening, because what else
did she not remember?

She took the down staircase, pausing when she got to the bottom. She was in a spectacular…living room? If so, it wasn't like any living room she'd ever seen. The arched ceiling soared three stories above her head. At one end was an enormous fireplace, while the wall at the other end was glass. Evidently he was fond of glass, because he had a lot of it. The view was literally breathtaking. But she didn't remember this, either. Any of it.

A hallway led off to the side, and cautiously she followed it. Something about this seemed familiar, at least, and she opened one door to discover the bathroom in which she'd showered last night—and in which he'd ripped off her clothes. Setting her jaw, she went in and looked around for her shoes. They weren't there. Resigned to being barefoot, she walked through the den, past the powder room she'd used and into the kitchen.

He was sitting at the bar, long legs hooked around a stool, a cup of coffee in one hand and the morning newspaper in the other. He looked up when she entered. "I found some tea, and the water is boiling."

"I'll drink water."

"Because tea is what you share with friends, right?" He put down the newspaper and got up, opening a cabinet door and taking down a water glass, which he filled from the faucet. "I hope you don't expect designer water, because I think it's a huge waste of money."

She shrugged. "Water's water."

He gave her the glass, then lifted his brows—both of them. "Cereal or bagel?"

"Bagel."

"Good choice."

Only then did she notice a small plate with his own bagel on it, revealed when he'd put down the paper. Maybe it was petty of her, but she wished they weren't eating the same thing. She didn't wish it enough to eat cereal, though.

He put a plain bagel in the toaster and got the cream cheese from the refrigerator. While the bagel was toasting, she looked around. "What time is it? I haven't seen a clock anywhere."

"It's ten fifty-seven," he said, without turning around. "And I don't own a clock—well, except for the one on the oven behind you. And maybe one on the microwave. Yeah, I guess a microwave has to have a clock nowadays."

She looked behind her. The oven clock was digital, showing ten fifty-seven in blue numbers. The only thing was, she'd been blocking the oven from his view—and he hadn't turned around, anyway. He must have looked while he was getting the cream cheese.

"My cell phone has the time, too," he continued. "And my computers and cars have clocks. So I guess I do own clocks, but I don't have just *a* clock. All of them are attached to something else."

"If small talk is supposed to make me relax and forget I hate you, it isn't working."

"I didn't think it would." He glanced up, the green in his eyes so intense she almost fell back a step. "I needed to know if you were Ansara, and to get the answer I was rough in the way I handled you. I apologize."

Frustration boiled in her. Half of what he said made no sense to her at all, and she was tired of it. "Just who the hell are these Aunt Sarah people, and where the hell are my *shoes?*"

Chapter 11

"The answer to the second part of your question is easy. I threw them away."

"Great," she muttered, looking down at her bare feet, toes curling on the cold stone tiles.

"I ordered a pair for you from Macy's. One of my employees is on the way with them."

Lorna frowned. She didn't like accepting anything from anyone, and she especially didn't like accepting anything from *him*—but it seemed she was having to do a lot of it no matter how she felt. On the other hand, he had thrown away her shoes and destroyed her blouse, so replacing them was the least he could do.

"And the Aunt Sarah people?" She knew he'd said "Ansara"—not that *that* made any more sense to her—but she hoped mangling the word would annoy him.

"That's a longer explanation. But after last night, you're entitled to hear it." A little *ding* sounded, and the toaster spat up the bagel. Using the knife he'd got to spread the cream cheese, he flipped the two bagel halves out of the toaster slot and onto a small plate, then passed knife, plate and cream cheese to her.

She took the bar stool farthest from him and spread cream cheese on one slice of bagel. "So let's hear it," she said curtly.

"There are a few other things I'd like to get cleared out of the way. First—" He reached into the front pocket of his jeans, pulled out a wad of bills and slid them in front of her.

Lorna looked down. Her license was tucked amid the bills. "My money!" she said, grabbing both and putting them in her own pockets.

"My money, don't you mean?" he asked grimly, but he hadn't insisted on keeping it. "And don't tell me again that you didn't cheat, because I know you did. I'm just not sure even *you* know you cheated, or how you're doing it."

She focused her attention on her bagel, her expression shutting down. He was going off into *woo-woo* land again, but she didn't have to travel with him. "I didn't cheat," she said obstinately, because he'd told her not to.

"You don't know— Hold on, my cell phone's vibrating." He pulled a small cell from his pocket, flipped it open and said, "Raintree… Yeah. I'll ask her." He looked at Lorna and said, "How much did you say your new shoes cost?"

"One twenty-eight ninety," she replied automatically, and took a bite of the bagel.

He flipped the phone shut and slid it back into his pocket.

After a few seconds the silence in the room made her look up. His eyes were such a brilliant green, they looked as if they were glowing. "There wasn't a call on my cell," he said.

"Then why did you ask—" She stopped, abruptly realizing what she'd said when he'd asked about the shoes, and what little color she'd regained washed out of her face. She opened her mouth to tell him that he must have mentioned the price of the shoes to her, then shut it again, because she knew he hadn't. She had a cold, sick feeling in the pit of her stomach, almost the same feeling she had every morning when she woke up. "I'm not a weirdo," she said in a thin, flat voice.

"The term is 'gifted.' You're gifted. I just proved

it to you. I didn't need any proof, because I already knew. I'm even more gifted than you are."

"You're crazy, is what you are."

"I'm mildly empathic, just enough that I can read people very well, especially if I touch them, which is why I always shake hands when I go into a business meeting," he said, speaking over her as if she hadn't interrupted. "As you know very well, using just my mind, I can compel people to do things against their wishes. That's a new one on me, but what the hell. We *are* close to the summer solstice. That, added to the fire, probably triggered it. I can do a bunch of different things, but most of all, I'm a Class A Number One Fire-Master."

"Which means what?" she asked sarcastically, to cover the fact that she was shaken to the core. "That you moonlight at the circus as a fire-eater?"

He held out his hand, palm up, and a lovely little blue flame burst to life in the middle of his hand. He casually blew it out. "Can't do that for very long," he said, "or it burns."

"That's just a trick. Stunt people do that in movies all—"

Her bagel caught on fire.

She stared at it, frozen, as the thick bread burned and smoked. He picked up the plate and flicked the burning bagel into the sink, then ran water on it. "Don't want the fire alarm to go off," he explained, and slid the plate, with the other half of bagel on it, back in front of her.

Behind him, a candle flared to life. "I keep a lot of candles around," he said. "They're my equivalent of a canary in a coal mine."

A thought grew and grew until she couldn't hold it back. "You set the casino on fire!" she said in horror.

He shook his head as he slid back onto his stool and picked up his coffee. "My control is better than that, even this close to the solstice. It wasn't my fire."

"So you say. If you're a Class A Number One hotshot Fire-Master, why didn't you put it out?"

"That's the same question I've been asking myself."

"And the answer is…?"

"I don't know."

"Wow, that's enlightening."

His brilliant grin flashed across his face. "Has anyone ever told you you're a smart-ass?"

She barely kept herself from flinching back in automatic response. Yeah, she'd heard the comment before—many times, and always accompanied by, or even preceded by, a slap.

She didn't look up to see if he'd noted anything strange about her response, but concentrated on putting cream cheese on the remaining half of her bagel.

"Since I had never done mind control before last night, it's possible I drained myself of energy," he continued after a moment. She still refused to look up, but she could feel the intensity of his gaze on her face. "I didn't feel tired. Everything felt normal, but until I explore the parameters, I won't know what the effects of mind control are. Maybe I wasn't concentrating as much as I should have been. Maybe my attention was splintered. Hell, I *know* it was splintered. There were a lot of unusual factors last night."

"You honestly think you could have put out that fire?"

"I know I could have—normally. The fire marshal would have thought the sprinkler system did a great job. Instead—"

"Instead, you dragged me into the middle of a four-alarm fire and nearly killed both of us!"

"Are you burned?" he asked, sipping his coffee.

"No," she said grudgingly.

"Suffering from smoke inhalation?"

"No, damn it!"

"Don't you think you should have at least a few singed strands of hair?"

He was only saying everything she'd thought herself. She didn't understand what had happened during the fire, and she didn't understand anything that had happened since then. Desperately, she wanted to skate over the surface of everything, pretend nothing weird was going on, and leave this house with the pretense still intact, but he wasn't going to let that happen. She could feel his determination, like a force field emanating from him.

No! she told herself in despair. No force field, no emanating. Nothing like that.

"I threw a shield of protection around us. Then at the end, when I was using all your power combined with mine to beat back the fire, the shield solidified a bit. You saw it. I saw it. It shimmered, like a—"

"Soap bubble," she whispered.

"Ah," he said softly, after a moment of thought. "So that's what triggered your memory."

"Do you have any idea how much that *hurt*, what you did?"

"Taking over your power? No, I don't know, but I can imagine."

"No," she said flatly. "You can't." The pain had been beyond any true description. If she said it had felt as if an anvil had fallen on her head, that would be an understatement.

"Again, I'm sorry. I had no choice. It was either that, or we were both going to die, along with the people still evacuating the hotel."

"You have a way of apologizing that says you'd do the same thing again if the situation arose, so it's really hard to believe the 'sorry' part."

"That's because you're not only a precog, though an untrained one, you're also very sensitive to the paranormal energy around you."

Meaning he *would* do the same thing again, in the same circumstances. At least he wasn't a hypocrite.

"Yesterday, in my office," he continued, "you were reacting to energies you wouldn't have sensed at all if you weren't gifted."

"I thought you were evil," she said, and savagely bit into the bagel. "Nothing you've done since has changed my mind."

"Because you turned me on?" he asked softly. "I took one look at you, and every candle in the room lit up. I'm not usually that out of control, but I had to concentrate to rein everything in. Then I kept looking at you and thinking about having sex, and damned if you didn't hook into the fantasy."

Oh, God, he'd known *that?* She felt her face burn, and she turned her embarrassment into anger. "Are you coming on to me?" she asked incredulously. "Do you actually have the *nerve* to think I'd let you touch me with a ten-foot pole after what you did to me last night?"

"It isn't *that* long," he said, smiling a little.

Well, she'd walked into that one. She slapped the bagel onto the plate and slid off the stool. "I don't want to be in the same room with you. After I leave here, I never want to see your face again. You can take your tacky little fantasy and shove it, Raintree!"

"Dante," he corrected, as if she hadn't all but told him to drop dead. "And that brings us to the Ansara. I was looking for a birthmark. All Ansara have a blue crescent moon somewhere on their backs."

She was so angry that a red mist fogged her vision. "And while you were looking for this birthmark on my *back* you decided to check out my ass, too, huh?"

"It's a fine ass, well worth checking out. But, no, I always intended to check it out. 'Back' is imprecise. Technically, 'back' could go from the top of your head all the way down to your heels. I've seen it below the waist before, and in the histories there are reports of, in rare cases, the birthmark being on the ass cheek. Given the seriousness of the fire, and the fact that I couldn't put it out, I had to make sure you hadn't been hindering me."

"Hindering you how?" she cried, not at all mollified by his explanation.

"If you had also been a fire-master, you could have been feeding the fire while I was trying to put it out. I've never seen a fire I couldn't control—until last night."

"But you said yourself you'd never used mind control before, so you don't know how it affected you! Why automatically assume I had to be one of these Ansara?"

"I didn't. I'm well aware of all the variables. I still had to eliminate the possibility that you might be Ansara."

"If you're so good at reading people when you touch them, then you should have known I wasn't," she charged.

"Very good," he acknowledged, as if he were a teacher and she his star pupil. "But Ansara are trained from birth to manage their gifts and to protect themselves, just as Raintree are. A powerful Ansara could conceivably have constructed a shield that I wouldn't be able to detect. Like I said, my empath abilities are mild."

She felt as if she were about to explode with frustration. "If I'd had one of these shields, you idiot, you wouldn't have been able to brain-rape me!"

He drummed his fingers lightly on top of the bar, studying her with narrowed eyes. "I really, *really* don't like that term."

"Tough. I really, *really* didn't like the brain-rape itself." She threw the words at him like knives and hoped they buried themselves deep in his flesh.

He considered that, then nodded. "Fair enough. Back to the subject of shields. You have them, but not the kind I'm talking about. The kind you have develop naturally, from life. You shield your emotions. I'm talking about a mental shield that's deliberately constructed to hide a part of your brain's energy. As for keeping me out—honey, there's only one other person, at least that I know of, who could possibly have blocked me from taking over his mind, and you aren't him."

"Ooooh, you're so scary-powerful then, huh?"

Slowly he nodded. "Yep."

"Then why aren't you, like, King of the World or something?"

"I'm king of the Raintree," he said, getting up and putting his plate in the dishwasher. "That's good enough for me."

Strange, but of all the really weird things he'd said to her, this struck her as the most unbelievable. She buried her head in her hands, wishing this day was over. She wanted to forget she'd ever met him. He was obviously a lunatic. No—she couldn't comfort herself with that delusion. She had been through fire with him, quite literally. He could do things she hadn't thought were possible. So maybe—just maybe—he really was some sort of leader, though "king" was stretching things a bit far.

"Okay, I'll bite," she said wearily. "Who are the Raintree, and who are the Ansara? Is this like two different countries but inhabited only by weirdos?"

His lips twitched as if he wanted to laugh. "Gifted. *Gifted*. We're two different clans—warring clans, if you want the bottom line. The enmity goes back thousands of years."

"You're the weirdo equivalent of the Hatfields and the McCoys?"

He did laugh then, white teeth flashing. "I've never thought of it that way, but…yeah. In a way. Except what's between the Raintree and the Ansara isn't a feud, it's a war. There's a difference."

"Between a war and a feud, yeah. But what's the difference between the Raintree clan and the Ansara clan?"

"An entire way of looking at life, I guess. They use their gifts to cheat, to do harm, for their personal gain. Raintree look at their abilities as true gifts and try to use them accordingly."

"You're the guys with the white hats."

"Within the spectrum of human nature—yes. Common sense tells me some Raintree aren't that far separated from some Ansara when it comes to their attitudes. But if they want to remain in the Raintree clan, they'll do as I order."

"So all the Ansara might not be totally bad, but if they want to stay in *their* clan, with their friends and families, they have to do as the Ansara king orders."

He dipped his head in acknowledgment. "That's about it."

"You admit you might be more alike than you're different."

"In some ways. In one big way, we're poles apart."

"Which is?"

"From the very beginning, if a Raintree and an Ansara crossbred, the Ansara killed the child. No exceptions."

Lorna rubbed her forehead, which was beginning to ache again. Yeah, that was bad. Killing innocent children because of their heritage wasn't just an opportunistic outlook, it was bad with a capital *B*. Part of her own life philosophy was that there were some people who didn't deserve to live, and people who hurt children belonged in that group.

"I don't suppose there has been much intermarriage between the clans, has there?"

"Not in centuries. What Raintree would take the chance? Are you finished with that bagel?"

Thrown off track by the prosaic question, Lorna stared down at her bagel. She had eaten maybe half of it. Even though she'd been starving before, the breakfast conversation had effectively killed her appetite. "I guess," she said without interest, passing the plate to him.

He dumped the bagel remnants and put that plate in the dishwasher, too. "You need training," he said. "Your gifts are too strong for you to go around unprotected. An Ansara could use you—"

"Just the way you did?" She didn't even try to keep the bitterness out of her tone.

"Just the way I did," he agreed. "Only they would be feeding the fire instead of fighting it."

As she stood there debating the merits of what he'd said, she realized that gradually she had become more at ease with discussing these "gifts" and that somewhere during the course of the conversation she had been moved from denial to acceptance. Now she saw where he was going with all this, and her old deep-rooted panic bloomed again.

"Oh, no," she said, shaking her head as she backed a few steps away. "I'm not going to let you 'train' me in anything. Do I have 'stupid' engraved on my forehead or something?"

"You're asking for trouble if you don't get some training, and fast."

"Then I'll handle it, just like I always have. Besides, you have your own trouble to handle, don't you?"

"The next few weeks will be tough, but not as tough for me as they will be for the people who lost someone. Another body was pulled out just after dawn. That makes two fatalities." His expression went grim.

"I'm not talking about that. I'm talking about the cops. Something hinky is going on there, because otherwise, why would two detectives be interviewing people before the fire marshal had determined if the fire was arson or accidental?"

The expression in his eyes grew distant as he stared at her. That little detail had escaped his all-knowing, all-seeing gifts, she realized, but if there was one thing a hard life had taught her, it was how the law worked. The detectives shouldn't have been there until it was clear there was something for them to detect, and the fire marshal wouldn't make that determination until sometime today, probably.

"Damn it," he said very softly, and pulled out his phone. "Don't go anywhere. I have some calls to make."

He'd meant that very literally, Lorna discovered when she tried to leave the kitchen. Her feet stopped working at the threshold.

"Damn you, Raintree!" she snarled, whirling on him.

"Dante," he corrected.

"Damn you, Dante!"

"Much better," he said, and winked at her.

Chapter 12

Dante began making calls, starting with Al Rayburn. Lorna was right: something hinky was going on, and he was pissed that she'd had to point it out to him. He should have thought of that detail himself. Instead of answering the detectives' questions, he should have been asking them his own, such as: What were they doing there? A fire scene wasn't a crime scene unless and until the cause was determined to be arson or at the very least suspicious. Uniformed officers should have been there for crowd control, traffic control, security—a lot of reasons—but not detectives.

He didn't come up with any answers to his

questions, but he hadn't expected to. What he was doing now was reversing the flow of information, and that would take time. Now that questions were being asked—by Al, by a friend Dante had at city hall, by one of his own Raintree clan members who liked life a little on the rough side and thus had some interesting contacts—a lot of things would be viewed in a different light.

Whatever was going on, however those two detectives were involved, Dante intended to find out, even if he had to bring in Mercy, whose gift of telepathy was so strong that she had once, when she was ten and he was sixteen, jumped into his head at a very inopportune moment—he'd been with his current girlfriend—and said, "Eww! Gross!" which had so startled him he'd lost his concentration, his erection *and* his girlfriend. Sixteen-year-old girls, he'd learned, didn't deal well with anything they saw as an insult to their general desirability. That was the day when he'd started blocking Mercy from his head, which had infuriated her at the time. She'd even told their parents what he'd been doing, which had resulted in a very long, very serious talk with his father about the importance of being smart, using birth control and taking responsibility for his actions.

Faced with his father's stern assurance that Dante *would* marry any girl he got pregnant and stay married to her for the rest of his life, he had then become immensely more careful. The Raintree Dranir most definitely did *not* have a casual attitude about his heirs. A Raintree, any Raintree, was a genetic dominant; any children would inherit the Raintree gifts. The same was true of the Ansara, which was why the Ansara had immediately killed any child born of a Raintree and Ansara breeding. When two dominant strands blended, anything could be the result—and the result could be dangerous.

Mercy's gift had only gotten stronger as she got older. Dante didn't think her presence would be required, though; the Raintree had other telepaths he could call on. They might not be as strong as Mercy, but then, they wouldn't need to be. Mercy was most comfortable at Sanctuary, the homeplace of the Raintree clan, where she didn't have to almost shut down her gift because of the relentless emotional and mental assault by humans who had no idea how to shield. Occasionally she and Eve, her six-year-old daughter, would visit him or Gideon—Mercy was completely female in her love of shopping, and he and Gideon were always glad to keep Eve the Imp while her mother indulged in some retail therapy—but Mercy was the guardian of the homeplace. Sanctuary was her responsibility, hers to rule, and she loved it. He wouldn't call for her help if he had other options.

The whole time he was making calls, Lorna stood where he'd compelled her to stay, fuming and fussing and growing angrier by the minute, until he expected all that dark red hair to stand straight up from the pressure. He could have released her, at least within the confines of the house, but she would probably use that much freedom to attack him with something. As it was, he had to admit he rather enjoyed her fury and less-than-flattering commentary.

The fact was, he enjoyed *her*.

He'd never before been so charmed—or so touched. When he'd heard that pitiful little whimpering sound she made in her sleep, he'd felt his heart actually clench. What really, really got to him was that it was obvious she knew what sound she'd been making—she probably did it all the time—and yet she resolutely denied it. *Snoring* his ass.

She refused to be a victim. He liked that. Even when something bad happened to her—such as himself, for instance—she furiously rejected any sign of vulnerability, any hint of sympathy, any suggestion that she was, in any way, weaker than King Kong. She didn't bother defending herself; instead she attacked, with a ferocious valiance and sharp tongue, as well as the occasional uppercut.

He'd been rough on her—in more ways than one. Not only had he terrified her, mentally brutalized her, he'd humiliated and embarrassed her by tearing off her clothes and examining her the way he had. If she'd only cooperated… But she hadn't, and he couldn't blame her. Nothing he'd done last night would have inspired trust in her, not that trust appeared to come easily to her in any case. He couldn't even tell himself that he'd never intended her any harm. If the blue crescent birthmark of the Ansara had been on her back—well, her body would never have been found.

The sharpness of his relief at not finding the birthmark had taken him by surprise. He'd wanted to take her in his arms and comfort her, though unless he bound her with a compulsion not to harm him, she would likely have taken his eyeballs out with her fingernails, and as for his other balls— he didn't want to think what she would have done to them. By that time she hadn't wanted anything from him except his absence.

The way she'd been allowed to grow up was a disgrace. She should have been trained in how to control and develop her gifts, trained in how to protect herself. She had the largest pool of raw energy he'd ever seen in a stray, which meant there was enormous potential for her to abuse or to be abused.

Now that he thought about it, her gift probably wasn't precognitive so much as it was claircognitive. She didn't have visions, like his cousin Echo; rather, she simply "knew" things—such as which card would be played next, whether a certain slot machine would pay off, how much her new shoes cost. Why she chose to play at casinos instead of buying a lottery ticket he couldn't say, unless she had instinctively chosen to stay as invisible as possible. Certainly she had the ability to win any amount of money she wanted, since her gift seemed to be slanted toward numbers.

Above all else, two sharp truths stood out:

She annoyed the hell out of him.

And he wanted her.

The two should have negated each other, but they didn't. Even when she annoyed him, which was often, she made him want to laugh. And he not only wanted her physically, he wanted her to accept her own uniqueness, accept him in all his differences, accept his protection, his guidance in learning how to shape and control her gift—all of which she rejected, which circled right back around to annoyance.

The doorbell rang, signaling the arrival of Lorna's shoes. Leaving her fuming, he went to the door, where one of his hotel staff waited, box in hand. "Sorry I'm late, Mr. Raintree," the young man said, wiping sweat from his forehead. "There was a wreck on the interstate that had traffic backed up—"

"No problem," he said, easing the young man's anxiety. "Thanks for bringing this out." Since he was continuing to pay his staff's salaries, he thought they might as well make themselves useful in whatever manner he needed.

He took the shoe box to the kitchen, where Lorna was still rooted to the spot. "Here you go, try them on," he said, handing the box to her.

She glared at him and refused to take it.

Guess he couldn't blame her.

He took the shoes from the box, the wads of tissue paper from the toes, and went down on one knee. He expected her to stubbornly refuse to pick up her foot, but she let him lift it, wipe his hand over her bare sole to remove any grit, and slide the buttery-soft black flat on her foot. He repeated the process with her other foot, then remained on one knee as he looked up at her. "Do they fit? Do they pinch anywhere?"

The shoes were much like her ruined ones, he knew: simple black flats. But that was where the resemblance ended. This pair was made of quality leather, with good arch support and good construction. Her other pair had had paper-thin soles, and the seams had been starting to fray. She'd been carrying over seven thousand dollars in her pocket, and wearing fifteen-dollar shoes. Whatever she was spending all that money on, clothing wasn't it.

"They feel okay," she said grudgingly. "But not a hundred and twenty-eight dollars worth of okay."

He laughed quietly as he rose to his feet and looked down at her face for a moment, charmed all over again by her stubbornness. She was one of those women whose personality made her prettier than she actually was, if one considered only her features. Not that she wasn't pretty; she was. Not flashy, not beautiful, just pleasant to look at. It was that attitude, that sarcastic, sassy mouth, the damn-you-to-hell-and-back eyes, that made her sparkle with vitality. The one way Lorna Clay would never be described was *restful*.

He should release her from the compulsion that kept her here, but if he did, she would leave—not just this house, but Reno. He knew it with a certainty that chilled him.

Dante functioned very well in the normal, human world, but he was the Raintree Dranir, and within his realm, he was obeyed. He had been Dranir for seventeen years now, since he was twenty, but even before that, he hadn't led an ordinary life. He was of the Raintree Royal Family. He had been Prince, Heir Apparent and then Dranir.

"No" wasn't a word he heard very often, nor did he care to hear it from Lorna.

"You may go anywhere you wish within this house," he said, and silently added a proviso that in case of danger, the compulsion was ended. If the house caught fire, he wanted her to be able to escape. After last night, such things were very much on his mind.

"Why can't I leave?" Her hazel green eyes were snapping with ire, but at least she didn't punch, pinch or kick him.

"Because you'll run."

She didn't deny it, instead narrowed her eyes at him. "So? I'm not wanted for any crimes."

"*So* I feel responsible for you. There's a lot you need to know about your gifts, and I can teach you." That was as good a reason as any, and sounded logical.

"I don't—" She started to deny she had any gifts, but stopped and drew a deep breath. There was no point in denying the obvious. When he had first broached the subject to her, in his office, her denial had been immediate and absolute. At least now she was beginning to accept what she was.

How had she come to so adamantly deny everything she was? He suspected he knew, but unless she was willing to talk about it, he wouldn't pry.

After a moment she said obstinately, "I'm responsible for myself. I don't want or need your charity."

"Charity, no. Knowledge, yes. I think I was wrong when I said you're precognitive." He watched relief flare on her face, then immediately die when he continued. "I think you may be claircognitive. Have you ever even heard of that?"

"No."

"How about *el-sike?*"

"That's an Arab name."

He grinned. *El-sike* was pronounced *el-see-kay*— and she was right, it did sound Arab. "It's a form of storm control. My brother Gideon has that gift. He can call lightning to him."

She gave him a pitying look. "It sounds like a form of brain damage. What fool wants to be near lightning?"

"Gideon. He feeds off electricity. He also has electrical psychokinesis, which in a nutshell means he plays hell with electronics. He explodes streetlights. He fries computers. It isn't safe for him to fly unless I send him a shielding charm."

Her interest was caught, however reluctantly. He saw the quicksilver gleam of it in her eyes. "Why doesn't he make his own shielding charms?"

"That's kind of along the same lines of precogs not being able to see their own futures. Only those in the royal family can gift charms, but never for themselves. He's a cop, a homicide detective, so I keep him stocked in protection charms, and if he has to fly, I send him a charm that shields his electrical energy so he won't fry all the plane's computers."

"Electrical psychokinesis," she said slowly, trying out the words. "Sounds kinky."

"So I've heard," he said dryly. He'd also heard that Gideon sometimes glowed after sex—or maybe that was before. Or during. Some things a brother just didn't ask too many questions about. But if Lorna was at last interested in learning about the whole range of paranormal abilities, he didn't mind using some of the more exotic gifts to keep her intrigued.

"Tell you what," he said, as if he'd just thought of the idea, when in fact he'd been considering something of the sort all morning. "Why don't you agree to a short trial period—say, a week—and let me teach you some basic stuff to protect yourself? You're so sensitive to every passing wave of energy that I'm surprised you're able to go out in public.

I can also set up some simple tests, get a ballpark idea of how gifted you are in different areas."

He saw the instant repudiation of that idea in her expression, a quick flash, then her curiosity rose to counter it. Almost immediately, caution followed;

she didn't easily put herself in anyone's hands. "What would I have to do?" she asked warily.

"You don't *have* to do anything. If you're absolutely dead set against the idea of learning more, then I'm not going to tie you to a chair and make you read lessons. But since you're going to be here for a few days anyway, you might as well use the time to learn something about yourself."

"I'll need my clothes," she said, which was as close to capitulation as he was likely to hear from her.

"Give me your address and I'll have them brought here."

"This is just for a few days. After that, I want your word you'll lift this stupid compulsion thing and let me go."

Dante considered that. He was the Dranir; he didn't, couldn't, give his word lightly. Finally he said, "After a week, I'll consider it. You're smart, you can learn a lot in a week. But I can't make a definite promise."

Chapter 13

"What, exactly, went wrong?"

Cael Ansara's tone was pleasant and even, which didn't fool Ruben McWilliams at all. Cousin or not, there had always been something about Cael that made Ruben tread very warily around him. When Cael was at his most pleasant, that was when it paid to be extra cautious. Ruben didn't like the son of a bitch, but there you go, rebellion made for strange bedfellows.

His intuition had told him to delay contacting Cael, so he hadn't called last night; instead, he'd put people in the field, asking questions, and his gamble had paid off—or at least provided an interesting variable. He didn't yet know exactly what they'd discovered, only that they'd found *something*.

"We don't know—not exactly. Everything went perfectly from our end. Elyn was connected to me, Stoffel and Pier, drawing our power and feeding the fire. She said they had Raintree overmatched, that he was losing ground—and fast. Then…something happened. It's possible he saw he couldn't handle the fire and retreated. Or he's more powerful than we thought."

Cael was silent, and Ruben shifted uneasily on the motel bed. He'd expected Cael to leap on the juicy possibility that the mighty Dante Raintree had panicked and run from a fire, but as usual, Cael was unpredictable.

"What does Elyn say?" Cael finally asked. "If Raintree ran, if he stopped trying to fight the fire, without his resistance it would have flashed over. She'd have known that, right? She'd have felt the surge."

"She doesn't know." He and Elyn had discussed the events from beginning to end, trying to pinpoint what had gone wrong. She *should* have felt a surge, if one had happened—but she not only hadn't felt a surge, she hadn't felt the retreat when the fire department beat back the flames. There *had* to have been some sort of interference, but they were at a loss to explain it.

"Doesn't know? How can she not know? She's a Fire-Master, and that was her flame. She should know everything about it from conception on."

Cael's tone was sharp, but no sharper than their own tones had been when he and Elyn had dissected the events. Elyn hadn't wanted the finger of blame pointed at her, of course, but she'd been truly perplexed. "All she knows is, just as she was drawing the fire into the hotel, she lost touch with it. She could tell it was still there, but she didn't know what it was doing." He paused. "She's telling the truth. I was linked to her. I could feel her surprise. She thinks there had to be some sort of interference, maybe a protective shield."

"She's making excuses. Shields like that exist only at homeplace. We've never detected anything like that on any of the other Raintree properties."

"I agree. Not about Elyn making excuses, but about the impossibility of there being a shield. She simply asked. I told her, no, I'd have known if one were there."

"Where were the other Raintree?"

"They were all accounted for." None of the other Raintree had been close enough for their Dranir to link to them and use their power to boost his own, as Elyn had done by linking to him and the others. They'd pulled in people to follow the various Raintree clan—members in Reno. There were only eight, not counting the Dranir, and none of them had been close to the Inferno.

"So, despite all your assurances to me, you failed, and you don't know why."

"Not yet." Ruben ever so slightly stressed the *yet.* "There's one other possibility. Another person, a woman, was with Raintree. None of us saw them being brought out because the fire engines blocked our view, but we've been posing as insurance adjusters and asking questions." They hadn't raised a single eyebrow; insurance adjusters were already swarming, and not just the ones representing Raintree's insurance provider. Multiple vehicles had been damaged. Casino patrons had lost personal property. There had been injuries, and two deaths. Add the personal injury lawyers to the mix, and there were a lot of people asking a lot of questions; no one noticed a few more people *or* questions, and no one checked credentials.

"What's her name?"

"Lorna Clay. One of the medics got her name and address. She wasn't registered at the hotel, and the address on the paperwork was in Missouri. It isn't valid. I've already checked."

"Go on."

"She was evidently with Raintree from the beginning, in his office in the hotel, because they evacuated the building together. They were in the west stairwell with a lot of other people. He directed everyone else out, through the parking deck, but he and this woman went in the other direction. Several things are suspicious. One, she wasn't burned—at all. Two, neither was Raintree."

"Protective bubble. Judah can construct them, too." Cael's tone went flat when he said Judah's name—Judah was his *legitimate* half brother and the Ansara Dranir. Envy of Judah, bitterness that he was the Dranir instead of Cael, had eaten at Cael all his life.

Ruben was impressed by the bubble. Smoke? Smoke had a physical presence; any Fire-Master could shield from smoke. But heat was a different entity, part of the very air. Fire-Masters, even royal ones, still had to breathe. To somehow separate the heat from the air, to bring in one but hold the other at bay, was a feat that went way beyond controlling fire.

"The woman," Cael prompted sharply, pulling Ruben from his silent admiration.

"I've seen copies of the statement she gave afterward. It matches his, and neither is possible, given what we know of the timetable. I estimate he was engaged with the fire for at least half an hour." That was an eternity, in terms of survival.

"He should have been overwhelmed. He should have spent so much energy trying to control the fire that he couldn't maintain the bubble. He's the hero type," Cael said contemptuously. "He'd sacrifice himself to save the people in the hotel. *This should have worked*. His people wouldn't have been suspicious. They would have expected him to do the brave and honorable thing. The woman has to be the key. She has to be gifted. He linked with her, and she fed him power."

"She isn't Raintree," said Ruben. "She has to be a stray, but they aren't that powerful. If there had been several of them, maybe there would have been enough energy for him to hold back the fire." He doubted it, though. After all, there had been four powerful Ansara, linked together, feeding it. As powerful as Dante undoubtedly was, adding the power of one stray, even a strong one, would be like adding a cup of water to a full bathtub.

"Follow your own logic," Cael said sharply. "Strays aren't that powerful, therefore she can't be a stray."

"She isn't Raintree," Ruben insisted.

"Or she isn't *official* Raintree." Cael didn't use the word "illegitimate." The old Dranir had recognized him as his son, but that hadn't given Cael precedence over Judah, even though he was the elder. The injustice had always eaten at him, like a corrosive acid. Everyone around Cael had learned never to suggest that maybe Judah was Dranir because of his power, not his birthright.

"She'd have to be of the royal bloodline to have enough power for him to hold the fire for that long against four of us," said Ruben dubiously, because that was impossible. The birth of a royal was taken far too seriously for one to go unnoticed. They were simply too powerful.

"So maybe she is. Even if the split occurred a thousand years ago, the inherited power would be undiminished."

As genetic dominants, even if a member of one of the clans bred with a human—which they often did—the offspring were completely either Ansara or Raintree. The royal families of both clans were the most powerful of the gifted, which was how they'd become royal in the first place; as dominants, their power was passed down intact. To Ruben's way of thinking, that only reinforced his argument that, no matter what, a royal birth wouldn't go unnoticed for any length of time, certainly not for a millennium.

"Regardless of what she is, where is she now?"

"At his house. He took her there last night, and she's still there."

Cael was silent, so Ruben simply waited while his cousin ran that through his convoluted brain.

"Okay," Cael said abruptly. "She has to be the

key. Wherever it comes from, her power is strong enough that he held the four of you to a draw. But that's in the past. You can't use fire again without the bastard getting suspicious, so you'll have to think of something else that'll either look accidental or can't be linked to us. I don't care how you do it, just do it. The next time I hear your voice, you'd better be telling me that Dante Raintree is dead. And while you're at it, kill the woman, too."

Cael slammed down the phone. Ruben replaced the receiver more slowly, then pinched the bridge of his nose. Tactically, killing the royal Raintrees first was smart. If you cut off the head of a snake, taking care of the body was easy. The comparison wasn't completely accurate, because any Raintree was a force to be reckoned with, but so were the Ansara. With the royals all dead, the advantage would be theirs and the outcome inevitable.

The mistake they'd made two hundred years ago was in not taking care of the royal family first, a mistake that had had disastrous results. As a clan, the Ansara had almost been destroyed. The survivors had been banished to their Caribbean island, where most of them remained. But they had used those two hundred years to secretly rebuild in strength, and now they were strong enough to once more engage their enemy. Cael thought so, anyway, and so did Ruben. Only Judah had held them back, preaching caution. Judah was a *banker*, for God's sake; what did he know about taking risks?

Discontent in the Ansara ranks had been growing for years, and it had reached the crisis point. The Raintree had to die, and so did Judah. Cael would never let him live, even in exile.

Ruben's power was substantial. Because of that, and because he was Cael's cousin, he'd been given the task of eliminating the most powerful Raintree of all—a task made more difficult because Cael insisted the death look accidental. The last thing he wanted was all the Raintree swarming to the homeplace to protect it. The power of Sanctuary was almost mystical. How much of it was real and how much of it was perceived, Ruben didn't know and didn't care.

The plan was simple: kill the royals, breach the protective shields around Sanctuary and take the homeplace. After that, the rest of the Raintree would be considerably weakened. Destroying them would be child's play.

Not destroying the Ansara homeplace two centuries ago, not destroying every member of the clan, was the mistake the Raintree had made. The Ansara wouldn't return the favor.

Ruben sat for a long time, deep in thought. Getting to Raintree would be easier if he was distracted. He and the woman, Lorna Clay, were evidently lovers; otherwise, why take her home with him? She would be the easier of the two to take out, anyway—and if she were obviously the target rather than Raintree, that wouldn't raise the clan's alarm.

Cael's idea had been a good one: kill the woman.

Chapter 14

Monday afternoon

"What happens if you die?" Lorna asked him, scowling as, car keys in hand, he opened the door to the garage. "What if you have a blowout and drive off the side of the mountain? What if you have a pulmonary embolism? What if a chicken-hauler has brake failure and flattens that little roller skate you call a car? Am I stuck here? Does your little curse, or whatever, hold me here even if you're dead or unconscious?"

Dante paused halfway out the door, looking back at her with a half amused, half disbelieving expression. "Chicken-hauler? Can't you think of a more dignified way for me to die?"

She sniffed. "Dead is dead. What would you care?" Then something occurred to her, something that made her very uneasy. "Uh—you *can* die, can't you?" What if this situation was even weirder than she'd thought? What if, on the *woo-woo* scale of one to ten, he was a thirteen?

He laughed outright. "Now I have to wonder if you're planning to kill me."

"It's a thought," she said bluntly. "Well?"

He leaned against the door frame, negligent and relaxed, and so damned sexy she almost had to look away. She worked hard to ignore her physical response to him, and most of the time she succeeded, but sometimes, as now, his green eyes seemed to almost glow, and in her imagination she could feel the hard, muscled framework of his body against her once more. The fact that, twice now, she'd felt his erection against her when he was holding her only made her struggle that much more difficult. Mutual sexual desire was a potent magnet, but just because she felt the pull of attraction, that didn't mean she should act on it. Sometimes she wanted to run a traffic light, too, because it was there, because she didn't want to stop, because she could—but she never did, because doing so would be stupid.

Having sex with Dante Raintree would fall into the same category: stupid.

"I'm as mortal as you—almost. Thank God. As much as mortality sucks, immortality would be even worse."

Lorna took a step back. "What do you mean, *almost?*"

"That's another conversation, and one I don't have time for right now. To answer your other question, I don't know. Maybe, maybe not."

She was almost swallowed by outrage. "What? *What?* You don't know whether or not I'll be stuck here if something happens to you, but you're going to go off and leave me here anyway?"

He gave it a brief thought, said, "Yeah," and went out the door.

Lorna leaped and caught the door before it closed. "Don't leave me here! Please." She hated to beg, and she hated him for making her beg, but she was suddenly alarmed beyond reason by the thought of being stuck here for the rest of her life.

He got into the Jaguar, called, "You'll be okay," and then the clatter of the garage door rising drowned out anything else she might have said.

Furious, she slammed the kitchen door and, in a fit of pique, turned both the lock on the handle and the dead bolt. Locking him out of his own house was useless, since he had his keys with him, but the annoyance value was worth it.

She heard the Jag backing out; then the garage door began coming down.

Damn him, damn him, *damn him!* He'd really gone off and left her stranded here. No, not stranded—*chained.*

Her clothes had been delivered earlier, and she'd changed out of the ruined pants—and out of his too-big silk shirt—so he wouldn't have had to wait for her to get ready or anything. He had no reason for leaving her here, given that he could easily prevent her from escaping with one of his damnable mind commands.

Impotently, she glared around the kitchen. Being a drainer—king—whatever the hell he'd said—had made him too big for his britches. He pretty much did whatever he felt like doing, without worrying about what others wanted. It was obvious he'd never been married and likely never would be, because any woman worth her salt would—

Salt.

She looked around the kitchen and spotted the big stainless steel salt and pepper shakers sitting by the cooktop. She began opening doors until she found the pantry—and a very satisfying supply of salt.

She'd noticed he put a spoonful of sugar in his coffee. Now she very carefully poured the salt out of the salt shaker, replaced it with sugar from the sugar bowl, then put the salt in the sugar bowl. He wouldn't much enjoy that first cup of coffee in the morning, and anything he salted would taste really off.

Then she got creative.

About an hour after he left, the phone rang. Lorna looked at the caller ID but didn't bother answering; she wasn't his secretary. Whoever was calling didn't leave a message.

She explored the house—well, searched the house. It was a big house for just one person. She had no frame of reference for estimating the square footage, but she counted six bedrooms and seven and a half baths. His bedroom took up the entire top floor, a vast expanse that covered more floor space than most families of four lived in. It was very much a man's room, with steel blue and light olive-green tones dominating, but here and there—in the artwork, in an unexpected decorative bowl, in a cushion—were splashes of deep, rich red.

There was a separate sitting area, with a big-screen television that popped out of a cabinet when a button was pushed and sank back into hiding afterward. She knew, because she found the remote and punched all the buttons, just to see what they would do. There was a wet bar with a small refrigerator and a coffeemaker in case he didn't want to bother going downstairs to make his coffee or get something to eat. She'd replaced the sugar with salt there, too—*and* mixed dirt from the potted plants in with his coffee.

Then she sat in the middle of his king-size bed, on a mattress that felt like a dream, and thought.

As big and comfortable as the house was, it wasn't what she would call a mansion. It wasn't ostentatious. He liked his creature comforts, but the house still looked like a place to be lived in, rather than a showcase.

She knew he had money, and a lot of it—enough to afford a house ten times the size of this one. Throw in the fact that he lived here alone, with no daily staff to take care of him and his home, and she had to draw the obvious conclusion that his privacy was more important to him than being pampered. So why was he forcing her to stay here?

He'd said he felt responsible for her, but he could feel that way wherever she stayed, and because of that damned newly discovered talent of his for making people do whatever he wanted, she couldn't have left if he'd commanded her to stay. Maybe he was interested in her untrained "power" and wanted to see what he could make of it just to satisfy his curiosity. Again, she didn't have to stay here for him to give her lessons or conduct a few experiments on her.

He wanted to have sex with her, so maybe that was what motivated him. He could compel her to come to him, to have sex, but he wasn't a rapist. He was possibly a lunatic, definitely a bully, but he wasn't a rapist. He wanted her to be willing, truly willing. So was he keeping her here in order to seduce her? He couldn't do that if he went off somewhere and left her here, not to mention doing so made her mad at him.

Somehow the sex angle didn't feel right, either. If he wanted to get her in bed, making her a prisoner wasn't the right way to win her over. Not only that, she wasn't a femme fatale; she simply couldn't see anyone going to such extraordinary lengths to have sex with her.

He had to have another reason, but damned if she could figure out what it was. And until she knew…well, there wasn't anything she could do, regardless. Unless she could somehow knock him out and escape, she was stuck here until he was ready to let her leave.

Last night, from the moment the gorilla had "escorted" her away from the blackjack table and manhandled her up to Raintree's office, had been a pure nightmare. One shock had followed so closely on the heels of another—each somehow worse than the one before—that she felt as if she'd lost touch with reality somewhere along the way.

Yesterday at this time she had been anonymous, and she liked it that way. Oh, people would come up and talk to her, the way they did to winners, and she was okay with that, but being alone was okay, too. In fact, being alone was better than okay; it was *safe*.

Raintree didn't know what he was asking of her, staying here, learning how to be "gifted." Not that he was asking—he wasn't giving her a choice.

He'd tricked her into admitting that she had a certain talent with numbers, but he didn't know how nauseated she got at the thought of coming out of the paranormal closet. She would rather remain a metaphysical garment bag, hanging in the very back.

He had grown up in an underground culture where paranormal talents were the norm, where they were encouraged, celebrated, trained. He had grown up a *prince*, for God's sake. A prince of weird, but a prince nonetheless. He had no idea what it had been like growing up in slums, skinny and unwanted and different. There hadn't been a father in her picture, just an endless parade of her mother's "boyfriends." He'd never been slapped away from the table, literally slapped out of her chair, for saying anything her mother could construe as weird.

As a child, she hadn't understood why what she said was weird. What was so wrong with saying the bus her mother took across town to her job in a bar would be six minutes and twenty-three seconds late? She had thought her mother would want to know. Instead she'd been backhanded out of her seat.

Numbers were her thing. If anything had a number in it, she knew what that number was. She remembered starting first grade—no kindergarten for her, her mother had said kindergarten was a stupid-ass waste of time—and the relief she'd felt when someone finally explained numbers to her, as if a huge part of herself had finally clicked into place. Now she had names for the shapes, meanings for the names. All her life she'd been fascinated with numbers, whether they were on a house, a billboard, a taxicab or anywhere else, but it was as if they were a foreign language she couldn't grasp. Odd, to have such an affinity for them but no understanding. She had thought she was as stupid as her mother had told her she was, until she'd gone to school and found the key.

By the time she was ten, her mother had been deep into booze and drugs, and the slaps had progressed to almost daily beatings. If her mother staggered in at night and decided she didn't like something Lorna had done that day or the day before—or the week before—it didn't matter—she would grab whatever was handy and lay into Lorna wherever she was. A lot of times Lorna's transition from sleep to wakefulness had been a blow—to her face, her head, wherever her mother could hit her. She had learned to sleep in a state of quiet terror.

Whenever she thought of her childhood, what she remembered most was cold and darkness and fear. She had been afraid her mother would kill her, and even more afraid her mother might not bother to come home some night. If there was one thing Lorna knew beyond doubt, it was that her mother hadn't wanted her before she was born and sure as hell didn't want her *after*. She knew because that had been the background music of her life.

She had learned to hide what numbers meant to her. The only time she'd ever told anyone—*ever*—had been in the ninth grade, when she had developed a crush on a boy in her class. He'd been sweet, a little shy, not one of the popular kids. His parents were very religious, and he was never allowed to attend any school parties, or learn how to dance, anything like that, which was okay with Lorna, because she never did any of that stuff, either.

They had talked a lot, held hands some, kissed a little. Then Lorna, summoning up the nerve, had shared her deepest secret with him: sometimes she knew things before they happened.

She still remembered the look of absolute disgust that had come over his face. "Satan!" he'd spat at her, and then he'd never spoken to her again. At least he hadn't told anyone, but that was probably because he didn't seem to have any buddies he *could* tell.

She'd been sixteen when her mother really did walk out and not bothered to come back. Lorna had come home from school—"home" changed locations fairly often, usually when rent was overdue—to find her mother's stuff cleared out, the locks changed and her own meager collection of clothes dumped in the trash.

Without a place to live, she had done the only thing she could do: she had contacted the city officials herself and entered the foster system.

Living in foster homes for two years hadn't been great, but it hadn't been as bad as her life had been before. At least she got to finish high school. None of her foster parents had beaten or abused her. None of them ever seemed to like her very much, either, but then, her mother had told her she wasn't likeable.

She coped. After she was eighteen, she was out of the system and on her own. In the thirteen years since then—for her entire life, actually—she had done what she could to stay below the radar, to avoid being noticed, to never, ever be a victim. No one could reject her if she didn't offer herself.

She had stumbled into gambling in a small way,

in a little casino on the Seminole reservation in Florida. She had won, not a whole lot, but a couple hundred dollars meant a lot to her. Later on she'd gone in some of the casinos on the Mississippi River and won some more. Small casinos were everywhere. She'd gone to Atlantic City but hadn't liked it. Las Vegas was okay, but too *too*: too much neon, too many people, too hot, too gaudy. Reno suited her better. Smaller, but not too small. Better climate. Eight years after that first small win in Florida, she regularly won five to ten thousand dollars a week.

That kind of money was a burden, because she couldn't bring herself to spend much more than she had always spent. She didn't go hungry now, or cold. She had a car if she wanted to pack up and leave, but never a new one. She had bank accounts all over the place, plus she usually carried a lot of cash—dangerous, she knew, but she felt more secure if she had enough cash with her to take care of whatever she might need. Unless and until she settled somewhere, the money was a problem, because how many savings books and checkbooks could she be expected to cart around the country?

That was her life. Dante Raintree thought all he had to do was educate her a little on her talent with numbers, and—well, what *did* he expect to happen? He knew nothing about her life, so he couldn't have any specific changes in mind. Was she supposed to become Little Mary Sunshine? Find other people like her, maybe develop their own little gated community, where, if you ran out of charcoal lighter fluid at the neighborhood barbecue, one of the neighbors could breathe fire on the briquettes to light them? Maybe she could blog about her experiences, or do talk radio.

Uh-uh. She would rather eat ground glass. She liked living alone, being alone and depending only on herself.

The phone rang again, startling her. She scrambled across the bed to look at the caller ID, though why she bothered, she had no idea; she wouldn't recognize the number of anyone calling Dante Raintree, anyway. She didn't answer that call, either.

She had sat on the bed, thinking, for so long that the afternoon shadows were beginning to lengthen, and she was drowsy. Thank goodness for that phone call, or she might have fallen asleep on his bed, and wouldn't that have been an interesting situation when he got home? She had no intention of playing Goldilocks.

But she *was* sleepy, as well as hungry. After a late breakfast, she hadn't had lunch. Why not eat a light dinner now and go to bed early? She couldn't think of any reason why she should wait for Raintree, since he hadn't had the courtesy to tell her when he might be back.

The least he could do was call—not that she would answer the phone, but he could always leave a message.

Definitely no point in waiting for him. She raided the refrigerator and made a sandwich of cold cuts, then looked at all the books in his bookshelves—he had a lot of books on paranormal stuff, but she chose a suspense novel instead—and settled down in the den to read for a while. By eight o'clock she was nodding over her book, which evidently wasn't suspenseful enough to keep her awake. The sun hadn't quite set yet, but she didn't care; she was still tired from the night before.

Fifteen minutes and one shower later, she was in bed, curled in a warm ball, with the sheet pulled over her head.

The flare of a lamp being turned on woke her. She endured the usual grinding fear, the panic, knowing that her mother wasn't there even though, all these years later, her subconscious still hadn't gotten the message. Before she could relax enough to pull the sheet from over her head, the covers were lifted and a very warm, mostly naked Dante Raintree slid into bed with her.

"What the hell are you doing?" she sputtered sleepily, glaring at him over the edge of the sheet.

He settled himself beside her and stretched one long, muscled arm to turn out the lamp. "There appears to be sand in my bed, so I'm sleeping here."

Chapter 15

"Don't be silly. I couldn't leave the house, so how would I get sand? It's salt." Maybe he expected her to deny any involvement, but that *would* be silly, given that she'd been the only person in the house after he left. Maybe he also expected her to get all indignant and starchy because he was in bed with her, but for some reason, she wasn't alarmed. Annoyed at being awakened, yes, but not alarmed.

"I stand corrected." He used his superior muscle and weight to shove her over in the bed. "Move over. I need more room."

He had already forced her out of her nice warm spot, which annoyed her even more. "Then why didn't you get in on the other side, instead of making me move?" she grumbled as she scooted to the other side of the bed, which was king-size, like every other bed in the house.

"You're the one who put salt in my bed."

The sheets were cold around her, making her curl in a tighter ball than usual. Even the pillow was cold. Lorna lifted her head and pulled the pillow from beneath her, tossing it on top of him. "Give me my pillow. This one's cold."

He made a grumbling sound, but pushed the warm pillow toward her and tucked the other pillow under his head. She snuggled down into the warmth; the soft fabric already had his scent on it, which wasn't a bad thing, she discovered. She had known him only a short time, but a lot of it had been spent in close contact with him. The primitive part of her brain recognized his scent and was comforted.

"What time is it?" she asked drowsily, already drifting back to sleep.

"You know what time it is. It's a number. Think about it." He sounded drowsy himself.

She had never thought of time as a number, but as soon as she did, the image of three numbers popped into her head. "One-oh-four."

"Bingo."

Mildly pleased, she went to sleep.

She woke before he did, which wasn't surprising, given how early she'd gone to bed and how late he'd gotten in. She lay there through the tense expectation of being hit, then slowly relaxed. The bed was toasty warm; he gave off so much heat that she could feel the warmth even though they weren't touching.

Sleepily curious to see if the time thing worked again, she thought of time as a series of numbers and immediately saw a four, a five and a one. She pulled the sheet from over her head; the room was getting a little brighter. Without any way to check—short of getting out of bed and going down to the kitchen, which she wasn't willing to do—she supposed four fifty-one was close enough. How handy was that, to not need a clock?

Dante was lying on his side, facing her, one arm bent under his head, his breathing slow and deep. The room was still too dim for her to make out many details, but that was okay, because she wasn't ready for details yet; the general impression was sexy enough as things were.

What was a woman supposed to think when a healthy, heterosexual man slept with her for the first time and didn't even try to cop a feel? That something was wrong with her? That he wasn't attracted to her?

She thought he was dangerously intelligent and intuitive.

Sex was definitely part of their relationship, if knowing someone for roughly thirty-six hours could be described as a relationship. Some of those thirty-six hours had seemed years long, especially the first four or five. She couldn't say that their time together had been quality time, either. On the other hand, since she hadn't seen him at his best, she thought she might know him better than someone who had known him for a much longer time but only in a social setting, so she wasn't surprised that he hadn't made a pass at her during the night.

She wasn't ready for sex with him, might never be ready, and he knew that. If he'd tried to storm the barricades, as it were, she would have stiffened her resistance. By simply sleeping with her and not making any overtly sexual moves, he was, in a way, counteracting those first terrible hours together and making sex a possibility, at least.

He wasn't even naked, though the boxers he'd worn to bed didn't cover much. She wasn't naked, either; he'd had *all* her clothes brought to her, so she was sleeping in her usual cotton pajamas. Perversely, because he *hadn't* tried to have sex, she began to wonder what it would be like if they did—then suspected that he'd known that would be her reaction.

Sex wasn't easy for her. She didn't trust easily; she didn't arouse easily. Voluntarily giving up her personal sense of privacy was difficult, and the payback was usually not worth the cost. She liked the feel of sex, and when she thought about it in the abstract, she wanted it. The reality, though, was that the execution didn't live up to the expectation. Regardless of what she was doing, she seldom relaxed completely, which she thought good sex probably required.

The thing was, she was more relaxed with Dante than she'd been in a long, long time. He knew what she was, knew she was different, and he didn't care—because he was even more different than she was. She didn't have to hide anything with him, because she didn't care if he liked her or not. She certainly hadn't tried to hide her temper or sweeten her tart tongue. Likewise, she had no soft-focus ideas about his character. She knew he was ruthless, but she also knew he wasn't mean. She knew he was autocratic, but that he tried to be considerate.

So maybe she could let herself go and really enjoy sex with him. She didn't have to worry about his ego; if he started going too fast, she could tell him to slow down, and if he didn't like that… tough. She wouldn't have to worry about his pleasure; he would see to that himself.

She wondered if he took his time, or if he liked to get down to business.

She wondered how big he was.

Maybe she could relax enough to enjoy it, and even if she didn't, at least she could satisfy her curiosity.

With a suddenness that startled her, he threw back the covers and got out of bed. "Where are you going?" she asked, surprised when he headed toward the door instead of the bathroom.

"It's sunrise," was all he said.

And? The sun rose every day. Did he mean he always got up at this time, even when he'd had only four hours' sleep? Or did he have an early appointment?

She didn't follow him. She had her own appointment—with the bathroom. She also wanted to give him enough time to have that first cup of coffee.

When she left her room forty-five minutes later, after having made the bed and put away her clothes, she went to the kitchen but found it empty. A pot of coffee had been made, however, and she smiled with satisfaction.

Where was he? In the shower?

She didn't intend to stand around waiting for him to make an appearance. She was in the living room, heading toward her bedroom, when he appeared on the balcony two floors above.

"Come up here," he called down. "I'll be outside."

His bedroom had a deck—or was it a balcony, too?—that faced east. She had looked at it yesterday, but hadn't gone out, because his damn command had kept her from stepping outside. There were two comfortable-looking chairs and a small table out there, and she'd thought it must be a comfortable place to sit in the afternoon when the sun had passed its apex and that side of the house was shaded.

She went up the two flights of stairs to his bedroom. His bed, she noticed, had been stripped; that gave her a sense of satisfaction. She could see him sitting in one of the chairs outside, so she went to the open French door. Coffee cup in hand, he sat with his head tilted back a little, his eyes almost closed against the brilliance of the bright morning sun, the expression on his face almost... blissful.

"You're handy with the salt, aren't you?" he said neutrally, sipping the coffee, but she sensed he wasn't angry. Of course, the coffee from the kitchen wasn't dirt-flavored. When he made the next pot of coffee in here, he might not be as sanguine about things.

"Payback."

"I guessed."

He didn't say anything else, and after a moment she shifted her weight. "Was that all you wanted, just to say that?"

He looked around, as if he'd drifted off into a

reverie and was faintly surprised by her presence. "Don't just stand there, come out here and sit down."

Just thinking about doing so gave her the sense of running into a wall. "I can't."

That got a quick smile from him as he realized she was still housebound. He didn't say anything, but immediately the mental wall disappeared.

"Crap," she said, stepping outside and going to sit beside him.

"What?"

"You didn't say anything, you just thought it. I'd hoped you had to speak the command out loud, that I had to *hear* it, before it would work."

"Sorry. All I have to do is think it. I was tempted to use the gift yesterday afternoon and tell a few people to go jump in the lake, but I restrained myself."

"You're a saint among men," she said dryly, and he gave her a quick grin.

"I was dealing with the media, so, considering the level of temptation, I tend to agree with you."

Media, huh? No wonder he had refused to take her with him.

"I called last night to tell you I wouldn't make it back until late, but you didn't answer the phone."

"Why would I? I'm not your secretary."

"The call was for *you.*"

"I didn't know that, did I?"

"I left a message for you."

"I didn't hear it." The answering machine was in the kitchen; she'd been in his bedroom when the last phone call came in, which must have been him calling her.

"That's because you didn't bother to play it back." He sounded annoyed now.

"Why would I? I'm not—"

"My secretary. I know. You're a pain in the ass, you know that?"

"I try," she said, giving him a smile that was more a baring of her teeth than anything related to humor.

He grunted and sipped coffee for a while. Lorna pulled her bare feet up in the chair and looked out over the mountains and broad valleys, enjoying being outside after an entire day cooped up in the house. The morning was cool enough to make her wish she had on socks, but not so cool that she was forced to go inside.

"Do you want to go with me today?" he finally asked, with obvious reluctance.

"Depends. What are you doing?"

"Overseeing cleanup, talking to insurance adjusters, and I still don't have an answer to why two detectives were asking questions immediately after the fire, so I'm pursuing that by going directly to the source."

"Sounds like fun."

"I'm glad someone thinks so," he said wryly. "Get ready and we'll eat breakfast out. For some reason, I don't trust the food here."

Chapter 16

Tuesday morning, 7:30 a.m.

The man sitting concealed behind some scrub brush had been in place since before dawn, when he had relieved the unlucky fool who had been on surveillance duty all night. When he saw the garage door sliding up, he grabbed the binoculars hanging by a strap around his neck and trained them on the house. Red brake lights glowed in the dimness of the garage; then a sleek Jaguar began backing out.

He picked up a radio and keyed the microphone. "He's leaving now."

"Is he alone?"

"I can't tell—no, the woman is with him."

"Ten-four. I'll be ready."

His job done for the moment, he let the binoculars fall before the light glinting on the lenses gave him away. He could relax now. Following Raintree wasn't his job.

"Has the fire marshal said yet how the fire started?" Lorna asked as they drove down the steep, winding road. The air was very clear, the sky a deep blue bowl. The shadows thrown by the morning sun sharply delineated every bush, every boulder.

"Only that it started around a utility closet."

She settled the shoulder strap of the seat belt so the nylon wasn't rubbing against her neck. "So have one of your mind readers take a peek and tell you what the fire marshal thinks."

Dante had to laugh. "You seem to think there are a lot of us, that I have an army of gifted people I can call on."

"Well, don't you?"

"Scattered around the world. Here in Reno, there are nine, including myself. None of them are gifted with telepathy."

"You mean you can't call your strongest telepath, tell him—"

"Her."

"—*her* the fire marshal's name, and she could do it from wherever she is?"

"The telepath is my sister, Mercy, and she could do it only if she already knew the fire marshal. If she were meeting him in person, she could do it. But a cold reading, at a distance of roughly twenty-five hundred miles, on a stranger? Doesn't work that way."

"I guess that's good—well, unless you need a stranger's mind read from a few thousand miles away. I suppose this means mind reading isn't one of your talents." She hoped not, anyway. If he'd read her mind that morning…

"I can communicate telepathically with Gideon and Mercy, if we deliberately lower our shields, but we're more comfortable with the shields in place. Mercy was a nosy little kid. Then, when she got older, she wanted to make sure we couldn't pop into her head without warning, so she armored up, too."

"What all *can* you do? Other than play with fire and this mind-control thing."

"Languages. I can understand any language, which comes in handy when I travel. That's called xenoglossy. Um…you know I have a mild empathic gift. Something that's fun is that I can make cold light, psycholuminescence. That's usually called witch light."

"Bet that comes in handy when the electricity goes off."

"It has on occasion," he admitted, smiling. "It was especially fun when I was a kid, and Mom made me turn out the light and go to bed."

That sort of home life was as alien to her as if he'd grown up on Mars, and it made her feel vaguely uneasy. To get away from the subject, she asked, "Anything else?"

"Not to any great degree."

She lapsed into silence, mulling over all that information. There was so much she didn't know about this stuff. From the way Dante talked about himself and his family, their gifts had evolved with age, and their skills had grown like any other skill, through constant use. If she began learning more about what she could do, would she find more abilities within her power? She wasn't certain she wanted that. In fact, she was almost certain she didn't. Enough was enough.

Now that she was away from his house, she felt exposed and vulnerable. Though his autocratic way of keeping her there had been maddening, maybe he'd had the right idea. She had been insulated from the world there, able to more calmly think about being one of the gifted—albeit a lowly "stray" rather than a Raintree or Ansara, which she likened to being a Volkswagen as compared to, well, a Jaguar—because she hadn't had to guard herself. With every minute they drew closer to Reno, and with every minute she grew more and more anxious. By the time he sent the Jaguar prowling up the on-ramp to the interstate and they joined with heavy traffic, she was almost in a panic.

Old habits and patterns were very hard to break. A lifetime of caution and secrecy couldn't be easily changed. What was easy enough to contemplate while in seclusion seemed entirely different in the real world. Lorna's mother hadn't been the only person in her life to react so negatively to her ability. Dante could call it a gift all he wanted, but in her life it had been more of a curse.

She felt suddenly dizzy and sick at just the thought of getting deeper into this new world than she already was. Nothing would change. If she let anyone know, she would be leaving herself open for exploitation at the best, ridicule or persecution at the worst.

"What's wrong?" Dante asked sharply, glancing over at her. "You're almost hyperventilating."

"I don't want to do this," she said, teeth chattering from sudden cold. "I don't want to be part of this. I don't want to learn how to do more."

He muttered a curse, gave a quick look over his shoulder to check traffic, and slotted the Jaguar between a semi and a frozen-pizza truck. At the next exit, he peeled off the interstate. "Take a deep breath and hold it," he said, as he pulled into the parking lot of a McDonald's. "Damn it, I should have thought—this is why you need training. I told you that you're a sensitive. You're picking up all the energy patterns around you—has to be all the traffic—and it's throwing you into overload. How in *hell* did you ever function? How did you survive in a casino, of all places?"

Obedient to his earlier suggestion, Lorna sucked in the deepest breath she could and held it. *Was* she hyperventilating? she wondered dimly. She supposed she was. But she was cold, so cold, the way she'd been in Dante's office before the fire.

He put a calming hand on her bare arm, frowning a little when he felt how icy her skin was. "Focus," he said. "Think of your sensitivity as this shining, faceted crystal, picking up the sun and throwing rainbows all around you. Envision it. Or if you don't like crystals, make it something else fragile and breakable. Are you doing that? Can you see it in your imagination?"

She struggled to concentrate. "What shape crystal? Hexagonal? How many sides does it have?"

"What difference does it—never mind. It's round. The crystal is round and faceted. Got it?"

She formed a mental picture of a round crystal, only hers was mirrored. It didn't throw rainbows, it threw reflections. She didn't mention that, though. Concentrating helped dispel that debilitating coldness, so she was willing to think of crystals all day. "Got it."

"Okay. A hailstorm is coming. The crystal will be shattered unless you build a shelter around it. Later you can come back and build a really strong shelter around it, but right now you have to use whatever materials you have at hand. Look around. What do you see that you can use to protect the crystal?"

In her mind she looked around, but no handy bricks and mortar were nearby. There were some bushes, but they weren't sturdy. Maybe she could find some flat rocks and start stacking them in layers to form a barrier.

"Hurry," he said. "You only have a few minutes."

"There are some rocks here, but not enough of them."

"Then think of something else. The hailstones are the size of golf balls. They'll knock the rocks down."

In her mind she glared at him; then, desperate and unable to think of anything else, she mentally dropped to her knees and began scooping a hole in the sandy dirt. The sides of the hole were soft and kept caving in, so she scooped some more. She could hear the storm approaching with a thunderous roar as the hail battered everything in its path. She had to get under shelter herself. Was the hole deep enough? She put the crystal in the hole, and hurriedly began raking dirt around and over it. No, it was too shallow; the crystal ball wasn't completely underground. She began raking dirt from a wider circle, piling it on top of the crystal. The first hailstone hit her shoulder, a blow like a fist, and she knew the dirt wasn't going to do the job. With no time left and no other choice, she threw her own body over the dirt mounded over the crystal, protecting it with her life.

She shook herself out of the image and glared at him. "Well, that didn't work," she snapped.

He was leaning very close, his green eyes intent on her face, his hand still on her arm. "What did you do?"

"I threw myself on the hand grenade, so to speak."

"What?"

"I was trying to bury the damn crystal but I couldn't get it deep enough, so I threw myself on top of it and the hailstones beat me to death. No offense, but your imagery sucks."

He snorted and released her arm, sitting back in his seat. "That wasn't my imagery, it was yours."

"You thought of the stupid crystal."

"Yeah. It worked, too, didn't it?"

"What did?"

"The imagery. Are you still feeling—I don't

know how you were feeling, but I'd guess it was as if you were being attacked from all sides."

Lorna paused. "No," she said thoughtfully. "I'm not feeling that now. But it wasn't as if I were being attacked. It was more of an anxious feeling, a sense of doom. Then I got so cold, just the way I did in your office before the fire."

"Only then? You've never felt overwhelmed like that except in my office?" He considered the idea, frowning a little.

She rubbed the back of her neck, feeling the knots of tension. "Contrary to what you seem to think, I could pretty much go anywhere and do anything without feeling all those swirls and currents, or like the world was coming to an end. I thought you were the one doing all of it, remember?" Whatever this new stuff was, she didn't like it at all. She wasn't a happy-go-lucky person, never had been—it was tough to be Little Miss Sunshine when you were getting slapped every time you opened your mouth—but neither had she felt hopeless, overwhelmed by a dark despair that went way beyond depression.

"I'm not a sensitive," he said. "I've never felt what you're describing. I know I give off a force field of energy, because other sensitives have picked up on it, but no one has ever said I made them feel as if the world was coming to an end."

"Maybe they didn't know you the way I do," she said sweetly.

"You're right about that," he replied, smiling a little, and just that fast the air between them became heavy and hot, as if a summer thunderstorm were approaching. His gaze dipped down to her breasts, stroked over the curves with an almost physical sensation. He'd never touched her breasts, hadn't touched her sexually at all unless she counted the times she'd been able to feel his erection against her. Come to think of it, that was pretty damn sexual. With a jolt of self-honesty, she realized she'd liked knowing she could make him hard; thinking of how he'd felt made her abdominal muscles clench, low in her belly.

How could he do that, make her respond so fast? Her nipples beaded, so that every breath she took scraped them against her bra, which made them even harder. She almost hunched her shoulders to relieve the pressure, but she knew that would be a dead giveaway. Her bra was substantial enough that he couldn't see her excitement, which was a good thing. He might suspect, from the heightened color she could feel in her cheeks, but he couldn't *know*.

His gaze flashed up, caught hers. Slowly, but not at all hesitantly, he lifted his hand and rubbed the back of one finger over her left nipple, letting her know that she'd been wrong: he *knew*. Her cheeks got hotter, and she felt that delicious clenching again, the softening deep inside. If she hadn't been thinking about having sex with him...if she hadn't been thinking just a couple of hours ago about seeing him naked...maybe she wouldn't have responded so readily. But she had been, and she did.

"When you're ready," he said, holding her gaze a moment longer. Then he dropped his hand and nodded toward the fast-food restaurant. "Let's go get breakfast."

He had his door open and was getting out when, in tones of astonishment, she said, "You brought me to get breakfast at *McDonald's?*"

"It's those golden arches," he said. "They get to me every time."

Chapter 17

"They're going into McDonald's," one of the Ansara watchers reported.

"Sit tight," said Ruben McWilliams, sitting on the bed in his motel room. Why the hell didn't motels put the damn phone on the stupid little table so a man could sit in a chair when he talked on the phone, instead of sitting hunched over on an uncomfortable mattress? "Keep them in sight, but don't get any closer. Something spooked him. Let me know when they leave."

Something had prompted Raintree to abruptly cut across two lanes of traffic and take the exit ramp at seventy miles an hour, but Ruben doubted it was a sudden urge for a McMuffin. It wasn't as if he couldn't have gone another couple of exits and found another McDonald's, without the dangerous maneuver.

He didn't think it was anything his people had done that had caused the aberrant behavior, but he wasn't on-site, so he couldn't be certain. His people were supposed to watch and follow, that was all. Raintree wasn't a clairvoyant, so he shouldn't have picked up any warning that way, but he could have had a premonition. Premonition was such a common ability, even ordinary humans had it. Raintree might have felt a twinge of uneasiness, but because he was one of the gifted, he would never dismiss the warning; he would act on it, where most ordinary humans would not.

Since there had been no immediate danger— that would come later—maybe he'd sensed an accident in his immediate future if he stayed on the interstate, so he'd gotten off at the next exit. That was possible. There were always variables.

Staging the planned incident hadn't been possible on such short notice. They hadn't known when Raintree would leave his house, or where he would go when he did. Now that they had a tail on him, they could direct the *amigos* to him wherever he was; then they would fall back and let the *amigos* do their job.

* * *

Over a McMuffin, Dante said, "Tell me exactly what you felt when you were in my office."

Lorna sipped her coffee, thinking. After the weird feelings she'd had in the car, she'd wanted something hot to drink, even though Dante had dispelled all the physical chill. The heat of the coffee couldn't touch the remnant of mental chill she still felt, but it was comforting anyway.

She searched through her memory. It was normally excellent anyway, but everything had happened so recently that the details were still fresh in her mind. "You scared the crap out of me," she finally replied.

"Because you'd been caught cheating?" he prompted when she didn't immediately go on.

"I didn't cheat," she insisted, scowling at him. "Knowing something isn't the same as cheating. But, no, it wasn't that. Once, in Chicago, I was going home one night and was about to take a shortcut through an alley. I used the alley a lot—so did a bunch of people. But that night, I couldn't. I froze. Have you ever felt a fear so intense it made you sick? It was like that. I backed out of the alley and took another way home. The next morning a woman's mutilated body was found in that alley."

"Presentiment," he said. "A gift that saved your life."

"I felt the same way when I saw you." She saw by his expression that he didn't like that at all, but he'd asked, so she told him. "I felt as if this huge force just…*slammed* into me. I couldn't breathe. I was afraid I'd pass out. But then you said something, and the panic went away."

He sat back in the booth, frowning. "You weren't in any danger from me. Why would you have such a strong reaction?"

"You're the expert. You tell me."

"My first reaction to *you* was that I wanted you naked. Unless you're terrified of sex, and I don't think you are—" he gave her a hooded look that had her nipples tightening again "—you weren't picking up anything from me that would cause you to feel that way."

Heat again pooled low in her belly, and it wasn't from the coffee. Because they were in McDonald's and there was a four-year-old sitting in the booth behind her, she looked away and forcibly removed her thoughts from going to bed with him. "At least part of it was from you," she insisted. "I remember thinking that even the air felt different, alien, something I'd never felt before. When you got closer, I could tell the feeling came from you. You're a dangerous man, Raintree."

He just watched her, waiting for her to continue,

because he couldn't accurately deny that particular charge.

"I could feel you," she said, her voice low as she became mired in the memory. "Pulling at me, almost like a touch. The candles were going wild. I wanted to run, but I couldn't move."

"I *was* touching you," he said. "In my imagination, anyway."

Remembering how she'd been snagged by his sexual fantasy, drawn in, stole her breath. "I knew something was wrong," she whispered. "I wasn't in control. I felt as if I'd been caught in a power surge that kept blinking out, and then coming back, pushing me off balance. Then I got so *cold*, just like in the car. Not a normal cold, with chill bumps and shivering, but something so intense it made my bones hurt. Then that feeling of dread came back, the same feeling I had in the alley. You were talking about how I was sensitive to the currents in the room—"

"I was talking about sexual currents," he said wryly. "The summer solstice is in a few days, and control is more difficult when there's so much sunshine. That's why the candles were dancing. I was turned on, and my power kept flaring."

Lorna thought about that. She'd been attracted to him from the first moment she'd looked him in the eyes. Regardless of the fear and panic she'd felt at first, when she had met his gaze, she'd fallen headlong into lust. The debilitating coldness had come afterward and hadn't affected her physical response to him, because when the coldness left, the attraction remained—unchanged.

"The cold went away," she said. "Like something had been pressing me into the chair and then suddenly was gone. I thought I might fall out of the chair, because I'd been pushing back so hard, and all of a sudden the pressure was gone. That was it. We talked some more, and then the fire alarm went off. End of scene, beginning of even more weirdness."

"And you felt the same thing in the car?"

She nodded. "Exactly the same. Except for the sex. The farther we got from the house, the more anxious and depressed I felt, as if I were really exposed and vulnerable. Then I got really cold."

"You were definitely picking up on external negative energies, probably from the traffic around us. You never know who's in the car beside you. Could be someone you wouldn't want to meet even on a crowded street at high noon. What puzzles me is why you felt the same way in my office." He shook his head. "Unless you sensed the fire that was about to burn down the casino, which is possible, if you have some precognitive ability."

"I think I might, but only as things relate to numbers." She told him about the 9/11 flight numbers, and the fact that she hadn't had any visions of airplane crashes or buildings burning, just the flight numbers interjecting themselves into her subconscious. "What I felt before the fire was *different*. Maybe it's because I'm—"

She stopped and glared at him. He raised his eyebrows. "You're…what?"

"I have a hang-up about fire." He waited, and, exasperated, she finally said, "I'm afraid of it, okay?"

"Anyone with any intelligence is cautious of fire. *I'm* cautious with it."

"It isn't caution. I'm *afraid* of it. As in terrified. I have nightmares about being trapped in a burning building." He might be cautious with fire, she thought, but it still turned him on. He would make a jim-dandy firebug. Standing in the burning casino, she had felt his fascination and appreciation for the flames, felt his excitement, because he had expressed it very physically. "Anyway, maybe that's why I felt so panicked then, and so anxious. But why would I feel that way today—unless you're going to force me into another burning building in the next hour or so, in which case tell me now, so I can kill you."

He laughed as he gathered up the debris of their meal, loading it on the plastic tray. She slid from the booth, walking ahead of him as they left the restaurant. "Where to now?"

"The hotel."

They were back on the interstate within a minute. Dante slanted a glance at her. "Feeling okay?"

"I feel fine. I don't know what was going on."

She *did* feel fine. She was riding around in a Jag with the most unusual man she'd ever met, and she was thinking about going to bed with him. She glanced over at him, thinking of how he'd looked wearing just those boxers, and feeling the pleasant warmth of anticipation.

She liked watching him drive. Sunday night, going to his house, she hadn't been in any shape to appreciate the smoothness, the economy of motion, with which he handled a car. Good driving was very sexy, she thought. The play of muscles in his forearms, bared by the short-sleeved polo shirt he was wearing, was incredibly sexy. He had to work out somewhere, on a regular basis, to keep that fit.

They were cruising in the middle lane. A car with a loud muffler was coming up from the right, and she saw him glance in the rearview mirror. "Idiots," he muttered, smoothly accelerating into the left lane. Lorna turned her head to see what he was talking about. A battered white Dodge, gray smoke belching from its exhaust, was coming up fast. She could see several people inside it. What had prompted Dante to move over and give them plenty of room was the blue Nissan right on the bumper of the Dodge.

"That's an accident waiting to happen," she said, just as the blue Nissan swung into the middle lane, the one they had just vacated, and shot forward until it was even with the white Dodge. The Nissan swerved toward the Dodge, and the driver of the Dodge slammed on his brakes, setting off a chain reaction of squealing brakes and smoking tires behind him. The Nissan's motor was screaming as the car drew even with Dante and Lorna. Inside, she could see four or five Hispanics, laughing and pointing back at the Dodge.

Traffic on the interstate was fairly heavy, as usual, but not so heavy that the driver of the white Dodge wasn't now rapidly gaining on them.

"Gangs," Dante said in a clipped voice, braking to let the rolling disaster that was unfolding get ahead of him. He couldn't go faster, because there was a car ahead of him; he couldn't get around the car, because the blue Nissan was right beside them, boxing him in. No one in the Nissan seemed to be paying attention to them; they were all watching the Dodge. If anything, the Nissan's driver let up on the gas pedal, as if he *wanted* the Dodge to catch up.

"Shit!" Dante swerved as far as he could to the left as the Dodge pulled even with the Nissan. Lorna saw a blur as the left rear passenger in the

Dodge rolled down his window and stuck out a gun; then Dante's right hand closed over her shoulder in a grip that seemed to go to the bone, and he yanked her forward and down as the window beside her head shattered in a thousand pieces. There were several deep, flat booms, punctuated by lighter, more rapid cracks, then a soul-jarring impact as Dante spun the steering wheel and sent them skidding into the concrete barrier.

Chapter 18

Somehow Dante had pulled her shoulder free of the seat belt's shoulder strap, but the lap belt tightened with a jerk. Something grazed the right side of her head and hit her right shoulder so hard and fast it slammed her backward, and she ended up facedown, with her upper body lying across the console and twisted between the bucket seats. All the horrible screeching noises of tires and crushed metal had stopped, and a strange silence filled the car. Lorna opened her eyes, but her vision was blurred, so she closed them again.

She'd never been in a car accident before. The sheer speed and violence of it stunned her. She didn't feel hurt, just…numb, as if a giant had picked her up and body-slammed her to the ground. The hurting part would probably arrive soon enough, she thought fuzzily. The impact had been so ferocious that she was vaguely surprised she was alive.

Dante! What about Dante?

Spurred by that urgent thought, she opened her eyes again, but the blurriness persisted and she couldn't see him. Nothing looked familiar. There was no steering wheel, no dashboard….

She blinked and slowly realized that she was staring at the backseat. And the blurriness was… fog? No—*smoke*. She heaved upward in abrupt panic, or tried to, but she couldn't seem to get any leverage.

"Lorna?"

His voice was strained and harsh, as if he were having difficulty speaking, but it was Dante. It came from somewhere behind and above her, which made no sense.

"Fire," she managed to say, trying to kick her legs. For some reason she could move only her feet, which was reassuring anyway since they were the farthest away; if they could move, everything between there and her spine must be okay.

"Not fire—air bags. Are you hurt?"

If anyone would know whether or not there was

a fire, Dante was that person. Lorna took a deep breath, relaxing a little. "I don't think so. You?"

"I'm okay."

She was in such an awkward position that pain was shooting through her back muscles. Squirming, she managed to work her left arm from beneath her and push with her hand against the back floorboard, trying to lift herself up and around so she could slide back into her seat. "Wait," Dante said, grabbing her arm. "There's glass everywhere. You'll cut yourself to shreds."

"I have to move. This position is murder on my back." But she stopped, because the mental image of what sliding across broken glass would do to her skin wasn't a good one.

There were shouts from outside, coming nearer, as passersby stopped and ran to their aid. Someone beat on Dante's window. "Hey, man! You okay?"

"Yeah." Dante raised his voice so he could be heard. She felt his hand against her side as he tried to release his seat belt. The latch was jammed; he gave a lurid curse, then tried once more. On the third try, it popped open. Freed from its restraint, he shifted around, and she felt his hands running down her legs. "Your right foot's tangled in the air bag. Can you move…" His hand closed over her ankle. "Move your knee toward me and your foot toward your window."

Easier said than done, she thought, because she could scarcely maneuver at all. She managed to shift her right knee just a little.

The man outside Dante's window grabbed the door handle and tried to pull it open, shaking the car, but the door was jammed. "Try the other side!" she heard Dante yell.

"This window's busted out," said another man, leaning in the front passenger window—or where it had been—and asking urgently, "Are you guys hurt?"

"We're okay," Dante said, leaning over her and pushing on her right ankle while he turned her foot.

The trap holding her foot relaxed a little, which let her move her knee a bit more. "This proves one thing," she said, panting from the effort of that small shift.

"Point your toes like a ballerina. What does it prove?"

"I'm definitely—*ouch!*—not precognitive. I didn't see *this* coming."

"I think it's safe to say neither of us is a precog." He grunted, then said, "Here you go." With one last tug, her foot was free. To the man leaning in the window he said, "Can you find a blanket or something to throw over this glass so you can pull her out?"

"I don't need pulling," Lorna grumbled. "If I can shift around, I'll be able to climb out."

"Just be patient," Dante said, turning so he

could slide his right arm under her chest and shoulders and support her weight a little to give her muscles some rest.

They could hear sirens blasting through the dry air, but still some distance away.

A new face, red and perspiring, and belonging to a burly guy wearing a Caterpillar cap, appeared in the broken window. "Had a blanket in my sleeper," he said, leaning in to arrange the fabric over the seat, then folding the excess into a thick pad to cover the shards of glass still stuck in the broken window.

"Thank you," Lorna said fervently as Dante began levering her upright into the seat. Her muscles were screaming from the strain, and the relief of being in a more natural position was so intense that she almost groaned.

"Here you go," said the truck driver, reaching through once more and grasping her under the arms, hauling her out through the broken window before she could do it under her own steam.

She thanked him and everyone else who had reached out to help, then turned and got her first look at the car as Dante came out with the lithe grace of a race car driver, as if exiting through a window was something he did every day.

But as cool and sexy as he made his exit look, what stunned her to silence was the car.

The elegant Jaguar was nothing but crumpled and torn sheet metal. It had skidded almost halfway around, the front end crushed against the concrete barrier, the driver's side almost at a T to the oncoming traffic. If another car had plowed into them after they hit the barrier, Dante would be dead. She didn't know why no other vehicle had smashed into them; traffic had been heavy enough that it was nothing short of a miracle. She looked at the snarled pileup of cars and trucks and SUVs stopped at all angles, as if people had been locking down their brakes and skidding. There was a three-car fender bender in the right lane, about fifty yards down, but the people were out of their vehicles examining the damage, so they were okay.

She wasn't okay. The bottom had dropped out of her stomach, and her heart felt as if someone had punched her in the chest. She had a very clear memory of Dante spinning the steering wheel, sending the Jaguar into a controlled skid—turning the passenger side away from the spew of bullets and his side toward the oncoming traffic.

She was going to kill him.

He had no right to take that sort of risk for her. None. They weren't lovers. They'd met less than forty-eight hours before, under really terrible circumstances, and for most of that time she would gladly have pushed him into traffic herself.

How dare he be a hero? She didn't want him to be a hero. She wanted him to be someone whose absence wouldn't hurt her. She wanted to be able to walk away from him, whole and content unto herself. She didn't want to think about him afterward. She didn't want to dream about him.

Her father hadn't cared enough to stick around, assuming he'd even known about her. She had no real idea who he was—and neither had her mother. Her mother certainly wouldn't have risked a nail, much less her life, to save Lorna from anything. So what was this...this *stranger* doing, putting his own life in danger to protect her? She hated him for doing this to her, for making himself someone whose footprint would always be on her heart.

What was she supposed to do now?

She turned her head, searching for him. He was only a few feet away, which she supposed made sense, because if he'd moved any farther away than that she would have been compelled to follow him. He wouldn't lift that damned mind control he used to shackle her, but he'd risk his life for her—the jerk.

He normally kept his longish black hair brushed back, but now it was falling around his face. There was a thin line of blood penciling down his left cheek from a small, puffy cut high on his cheekbone. The skin around the wound was swelling and turning dark. His left arm looked bruised, too; the span from his wrist almost to his elbow was a dark red. He wasn't cradling his arm or swiping at his cheek, any of the things people instinctively did when they were hurt. His injuries might as well not exist for all the attention he paid them.

He looked in complete command of himself and the situation.

Lorna thought she might be sick, she was so angry. What he'd done wasn't fair—not that he'd seemed concerned about fairness before now anyway.

As if he were attuned to her thoughts, his head turned sharply and his gaze zeroed in on her. With two swift strides he was beside her, taking her arm. "You don't have any color at all in your face. You should sit down."

"I'm fine," she said automatically. A sudden breeze blew a curtain of hair across her face, and she lifted her hand to push it back. Two RPD patrol cars were approaching on the other side of the highway, sirens blaring, and she almost had to shout to make herself heard. "I'm not hurt."

"No, but you've had a shock." He raised his voice, too, turning his head to watch the patrol cars come to a stop on the other side of the barrier. The sirens died, but other emergency vehicles were approaching, and the din was getting louder again.

"I'm *okay!*" she insisted, and she was—physically, at least.

His hand closed on her arm, moving her toward the concrete barrier. "Come on, sit down. I'll feel better if you do."

"I'm not the one bleeding," she pointed out.

He touched his cheek, as if he'd forgotten all about the cut, or maybe had never noticed it in the first place. "Then come sit down with me and keep me company."

As it happened, neither of them got to sit down. The cops were trying to find out what had happened, get traffic straightened out and moving again, albeit very slowly, and get any injured people transported to a hospital to be checked out. Soon a total of seven patrol cars were on the scene, along with a fire engine and three medic trucks. The drivers of the damaged cars that were still drivable were instructed to move their vehicles to the shoulder.

There were several witnesses to what had happened. No one knew whether road rage had caused the shooting or if the whole thing had been a conflict between rival gangs, but everyone had an opinion and a slightly different version of events. The one thing they all agreed on was that the people in the white Dodge had been shooting at the Nissan, and the people in the Nissan had been shooting back.

"Did anyone get the plate number of either vehicle?" a patrolman asked.

Dante immediately looked at Lorna. "Numbers?"

She thought of the white Dodge and three numbers came into sharp focus. "The Dodge is 873." Nevada plates were three digits followed by three letters.

"Did you get the letters?" the patrolman asked, pen at the ready.

Lorna shook her head. "I just remember the numbers."

"This will narrow the search considerably. What about the Nissan?"

"Hmm…612."

He jotted that down, too, then turned away as he got on the radio.

Dante's cell phone rang. He fished it from the front pocket of his jeans and checked the caller ID. "It's Gideon," he said, flipping the phone open. "What's up?" He listened a moment, then said, "Royally screwed."

A brief pause. "I remember."

They talked for less than a minute when Lorna heard him say, "A glimpse of the future," which made her wonder what was going on. He had just laughed at something his brother said when she suddenly shivered, wrapping her arms around herself even though the temperature was rapidly climbing toward the nineties. That awful, bone-aching chill had seized her as suddenly as if she'd been dropped into a pool of ice water.

Dante's gaze sharpened, and he abruptly ended the call, tucking the phone back into his pocket.

"What's wrong?" he asked, keeping his tone low as he pulled her to the side.

She fought waves of dizziness, brought on by the intense cold. "I think the depraved serial killer must have followed us," she said.

Chapter 19

Dante put his arms around her, pulling her against the heat of his body. His body temperature was always high, she thought, as if he had a permanent fever. That heat felt wonderful now, warming her chilled skin.

"Focus," he said, bending his head so no one else could hear him. "Think of building that shelter."

"I don't want to build a damn shelter," she said fretfully. "This didn't happen before I met you, and I want it to stop."

He rubbed his cheek against her hair, and she felt his lips move as he smiled. "I'll see what I can do. In the meantime, if you don't want to build shelters, see if you can tell what's causing the problem. Close your eyes, mentally search around us, and tell me if you're picking up anything, like any changes in energy patterns from a particular area."

That suggestion seemed a lot more practical to her than building imaginary shelters for imaginary mirrored crystals. She would rather be doing something to stop these sudden sick feelings instead of merely learning how to handle them. She did as he said, leaning into him and letting him support part of her weight while she closed her eyes and began mentally searching for something weird. She didn't know what she was doing, or what she was "looking" for, but she felt better for doing it.

"Is this really supposed to work?" she asked against his shoulder. "Or are you just distracting me?"

"It should work. Everyone has a personal energy field, but some are stronger than others. A sensitive has a heightened awareness of these energy fields. You should be able to tell where a strong one is coming from, sort of like being able to tell from which direction the wind is blowing."

That made sense to her, put it in terms she could understand. The thing was, *if* she was a sensitive, why didn't she sense stuff like this on a regular basis? Other than the time in Chicago when she'd been suddenly terrified of what lurked in that alley, she'd never been aware of anything unusual.

Some are stronger than others, Dante had said. Maybe she had been around mostly normal people all her life. If so, these feelings must mean that there were now people near her who weren't normal and had very strong energy fields.

The strongest of all was holding her in his arms. Concentrating like this, she decided to use him as a sort of standard, a pattern, against which she could measure anything else she detected. She could physically *feel* the energy of his gifts, almost like static electricity surrounding her entire body. The sensation was too strong to call pleasant, but it wasn't *un*pleasant. Rather, it was exciting and sexual, like tiny pinpoints of fire reaching deep into her body.

Keeping a part of the feeling in the forefront of her consciousness, she began widening her awareness, looking for the places that had stronger currents. It was, she thought, like trout fishing.

At first there was nothing other than a normal flow of energy, albeit from many different people. She and Dante were surrounded by police officers, firemen, medics, people who had come to their aid. Their energy flow was warm and comforting, concerned, protective. These were good people; they all had their quirks, but their baseline was good.

She expanded her mental circle. The pattern here was slightly different. These were the onlookers, the rubberneckers, the ones who were curious but weren't moved to help. They wanted to talk about seeing the accident, about being stuck in traffic for X number of hours, as if it were a great hardship to endure, but they didn't want to put out any effort. They—

There!

She started, a little alarmed by what she felt.

"Where is it?" Dante whispered against her hair, his arms tightening. Probably the people around them thought he was comforting her, or that they were clinging to each other in gratitude that they'd been spared any harm.

She didn't open her eyes. "To my left. About…I don't know…a hundred yards out, maybe. Off to the side, as if he's pulled onto the shoulder."

"He?"

"He," she replied, very definitely.

"Our friends missed completely," the Ansara follower said in disgust, lowering the binoculars he held in one hand to concentrate on the phone call. "He wrecked the car, but they aren't hurt."

Ruben cursed under his breath. He guessed this just proved the old adage: *If you want something done right, do it yourself.*

"Call off surveillance," he said. "I have something else in mind."

Their plans had been too complex. The best plan was the simplest plan. There were fewer details that could go wrong, fewer people to screw things up, less chance of the target being warned.

Instead of trying to make Raintree's death look like an accident, the easiest thing to do was wait until the last minute, when it was too late for the clan to rally to Sanctuary, then simply put a bullet through his head.

Simple was always best.

"I see who you're talking about," Dante said, "but I can't tell anything from this distance. He doesn't seem to be doing anything, just standing outside his car like a bunch of other people."

"Watching," Lorna said. "He's watching us."

"Can you tell anything about his energy field?"

"He's sending out a lot of waves. He's stronger than anything else I'm sensing out there, but, um, I'd say nowhere near as strong as you." She lifted her head and opened her eyes. "He's the only unusual one as far as I can tell. Are you sure I'm not just imagining this?"

"I'm sure. You need to start trusting your senses. He's probably just—"

"Mr. Raintree," one of the policemen called, beckoning Dante over.

He gave Lorna a quick kiss on the mouth, then

released her and strode over to the cop. Willy-nilly, Lorna followed, though she stopped as soon as she was able, when the compulsion was no longer tugging her forward.

The accident scene was beginning to clear up; witnesses had given their statements, and more and more people were managing to maneuver their vehicles around the demolished Jag, the remains of the fender bender and all the rescue vehicles. Two wreckers had arrived, one to tow Dante's Jaguar, the other to get the center car in the fender bender, because it had a ruptured radiator. Before his poor car was taken away, Dante was getting his registration and insurance card from the glove compartment, as well as the garage door opener. Given how mangled the car was, finding anything and getting to it was a major undertaking.

From what Lorna could tell, he wasn't upset at all about the Jaguar. He didn't like the inconvenience, but the car itself didn't mean anything to him. He had already made arrangements for a rental car to be waiting for him at the hotel, and one of his many employees was on the way to the accident site to pick them up. As she had always suspected, money smoothed out many of life's bumps.

Thinking of money prompted her to casually brush her hand against her left front pocket. Her money was still there, and her driver's license and the tiny pair of scissors were in her right pocket. She had no idea what good those scissors would do in any truly dangerous situation, but she had them anyway.

She noticed she was feeling much better, that the ugly, cold sensation had gone away. She turned and looked over to where the watcher had been parked. He wasn't there any longer, and neither was his car. Coincidence, she wondered, or cause and effect?

And wasn't it odd that she'd had that sickening cold feeling both right before the casino fire, and right before she almost got mowed down in the crossfire of a gang shooting? Maybe she wasn't reacting to a person at all but to something that was about to happen. Maybe that coldness was a warning. Of course, she'd also gotten the feeling right before Dante fed her a McMuffin for breakfast, but the principle could still be holding true: Warning! McMuffin ahead!

She had almost come to terms with the clair-cognizance thing, because even though she'd spent a lifetime insisting she was simply good with numbers, she had always *known* it was more than that. She didn't want to discover yet another talent, particularly one that seemed to be useless. A warning was all well and good if you knew what you were being warned about. Otherwise, why bother?

"Our ride's here," Dante said, coming up behind

her and resting his hand on the curve of her waist. "Do you want to go to the hotel with me, or go back home?"

Home? He was referring to his house as her home? She looked up, ready to nail him on his mistake, and the words died on her lips. He was watching her with a steady, burning intent; that hadn't been a slip of the tongue but a warning of a different kind.

"We both know where we're going with this," he said. "I have a suite at the hotel, and the electricians got the power back on yesterday, so it's functional. You can come with me to the hotel or go home, but either way, you're going to be under me. The only difference is that going home will give you a little more time, if you need it."

She needed more than time, but standing on the side of the interstate wasn't the place to have the showdown she knew was coming.

"I haven't decided yet whether or not to sleep with you, and I'll make the decision on my timetable, not yours," she said. "I'll come to the hotel with you because I don't want to spend another day cooped up in that house, so don't get too cocky, Raintree."

The expression of intense focus faded, to be replaced by wryness. Looking down at himself, he said, "Too late."

Chapter 20

Lorna was too restless to just sit in Dante's suite while he was literally all over the hotel, directing the cleaning and repairs, touring with insurance adjusters, meeting with contractors. She dogged his steps, listening but not joining in. The behind-the-scenes details of a luxury hotel were fascinating. The place was hopping, too. Rather than wait until the insurance companies ponied up, he'd brought the adjusters in to take pictures; then he got on with the repairs using his own money.

That he was able to do so told her that he was seriously wealthy, which made his lifestyle even more of a statement about him. He didn't have an army of servants waiting on him. He lived in a big, gorgeous home, but it wasn't a mansion. He drove expensive cars, but he drove himself. He made his own breakfast, loaded his own dishwasher. He liked luxury but was comfortable with far less.

When it came to the hotel, though, he was unbending. Everything had to be top notch, from the toilet paper in the bathrooms to the sheets on the beds. A room that was smoke-damaged couldn't be cleaned and described as "good enough." It had to be perfect. It had to be better than it had been before the fire. If the smell of smoke wouldn't come out of the curtains, the curtains were discarded; likewise the miles of carpet.

Lorna found out that the day before had been a madhouse, with guests being allowed to go to their rooms and retrieve their belongings. Because the destroyed casino was attached to the hotel, for liability purposes guests had to be escorted to make certain their curiosity didn't lead them where they shouldn't go.

A casino existed for one reason only, and that reason was money. In a rare moment when he had time to talk, he told Lorna that over six million dollars a day had to go through the casino just for him to break even, and since the whole point of a casino was its generous profit margin, the amount of cash he actually dealt with on a daily basis was mind-boggling.

The acre of melted and charred slot machines held thousands upon thousands of dollars, so the ruins had to have around-the-clock security until the machines could be transported and as much as possible of their contents was salvaged. About half the machines had spewed printed tickets instead of belching out quarters, which saved both time and money. The coin vaults and the master vault were fireproof, thus saving that huge amount of cash, and his cashiers in the cages had refused to evacuate until they secured the money, which had been very loyal of them but not smart: the two fatalities had been from their ranks.

The fire marshal was wrapping up his investigation, so Dante cornered him. "Was it arson?" he demanded bluntly.

"All indications are that it was electrical in nature, Mr. Raintree. I haven't found any trace of accelerants at the source of the fire. The flames reached unusually high temperatures, so I was suspicious, I admit."

"So was I—when detectives were here questioning me immediately after the fire on Sunday night, when you hadn't even begun your investigation. This wasn't a crime scene."

The fire marshal rubbed his nose. "They didn't

tell you? A call came in about the time the fire started. Some nutcase claimed he was burning down the casino. When they tracked him down, turns out he'd been eating in one of the restaurants, and when the fire alarm went off, he pulled out his trusty cell phone and made a grab for glory. He'd had one too many adult beverages." He shook his head. "Some people are nuts."

Dante met Lorna's gaze; both were rueful. "We'd wondered what was going on. I was beginning to feel like a conspiracy theorist," he said.

"Weird things happen in fires. One of them is how you two are alive. You had no protection at all, but the heat and smoke didn't get to you. Amazing."

"I felt as if the smoke got to us," Dante said in a dry tone. "I thought I was coughing up my lungs."

"But your airways had no significant damage. I've seen people die who faced less smoke than you two dealt with."

Lorna wondered what he would think if he could see what was left of Dante's Jaguar, since the two of them were walking around without even a bruise.

No, that wasn't right. Frowning, she looked at Dante, really looked. He'd had a cut on his face where the impact of the air bag had literally split open the skin over his cheekbone. His cheekbone had been bruised and was swelling, and his left arm had been bruised.

Just a few hours later, his cheek looked fine. She couldn't see the cut at all. There was no swelling, no bruising. She knew she hadn't imagined it, because there had been blood on his shirt, and he had gone to his suite to change; instead of the polo shirt, he now wore a white dress shirt with his jeans, the sleeves rolled up to expose his unbruised left forearm.

She didn't have any bruises, either. After the way she'd been slammed around, she should at least have some stiff and sore muscles, but she felt fine. *What was going on?*

"That was a dead end," he remarked after the fire marshal had left and he was inspecting the damage done to the landscaping. "The stupidity of some people is mind-boggling."

"I know," she said absently, still mentally chasing the mystery of the vanishing cut. Was there any way to diplomatically ask a man, *Are you human?*

But what about her own lack of bruises? She knew *she* was human. Was this part of his repertoire? Had he somehow kept her from being injured?

"The cut on your face," she blurted, too troubled to keep the words in. "What happened to it?"

"I'm a fast healer."

"Don't pull that crap on me," she said, more annoyed than was called for. "Your cheekbone was bruised and swollen, and the skin was split open just a few hours ago. Now there isn't a single mark."

He gave her expression a lightning fast assessment, then said, "Let's go up to the suite so we can talk. There are a few things I haven't mentioned."

"No joke," she muttered as they went through the hotel offices to his private elevator, which went only to his suite. His office was on the same floor, but it was separate from the suite, on the other side of the hotel. When his chief of security had dragged her up here, he had used one of the public elevators. No wonder there hadn't been any other people on the floor when they evacuated, she thought; the entire floor was his.

The three-thousand-square-foot suite felt and looked like any luxury hotel suite: completely impersonal. He'd said the only time he spent the night there was if some complication kept him at the casino so late that driving home was ridiculous. The rooms were large and comfortable, but there was nothing of him there except the changes of clothing he kept for emergencies.

It was strange, she thought, that she already knew his taste in furnishings, his color choices, artwork he had personally chosen. Some interior designer specializing in hotels, not in homes, had decorated this suite.

He strolled down the two steps to the sunken living room and over to the windows. He had an affinity for windows, she'd noticed. He liked glass, and lots of it—but he liked being outside even more, which was why the suite had a sun-drenched balcony large enough to hold a table and chairs for alfresco dining.

"Okay," she said, "now tell me how bruises and cuts went away in just a few hours. And while you're at it, tell me why I'm not bruised, too. I'm not even sore!"

"That one's easy," he said, pulling a silver charm from his pocket and draping the cord over his hand so the charm lay flat on his palm. "This was in the console."

The little charm was some sort of bird in flight, maybe an eagle. She shook her head. "I don't get it."

"It's a protection charm. I told you about them. I keep Gideon supplied with them. He usually sends me fertility charms—"

Lorna jerked back, making a cross with her fingers as if to ward off a vampire. "Keep that thing away from me!"

He chuckled. "I said it's a protection charm, not a fertility charm."

"You mean it's like a rubber you hang around your neck instead of putting on your penis?"

"Not that kind of protection. This kind prevents physical harm—or minimizes the damage."

"You think that's why we weren't injured today?"

"I know it is. Since he's a cop, Gideon wears one

all the time. This one came in the mail on Saturday, which means he'd just made it. I don't know why he made a protection charm instead of a fertility charm, unless he now has a diabolical plot to eventually disguise a fertility charm as a protection charm, but this one is the real deal. This close to the solstice, his gifts can get away from him, just like mine sometimes do. He must have breathed one hell of a charm," he said admiringly. "I didn't wear it. I just put it in the glove box and forgot about it. Normally the charms are for specific individuals, but when neither of us was injured today…I guess it must affect anyone within a certain distance. It's the only explanation."

Actually, that was kind of cool. She even liked the way he'd phrased it: *Breathed one hell of a charm.* "Does it make you heal faster, too?"

Dante shook his head as he slipped the charm back in his pocket. "No, that's just part of being Raintree. When I say I'm a fast healer, I mean really, really fast. A little cut like that—it was nothing. A deeper cut might take all night."

"How terrible for you," she said, scowling at him. "What other unfair advantages do you have?"

"We live longer than most humans. Not a lot longer, but our average life expectancy is about ninety to a hundred years. They're usually good years, too. We tend to stay really healthy. For instance, I've never had a cold. We're immune to viruses. Bacterial infections can still lay us low, but viruses basically don't recognize our cellular composition."

Of all the things he'd told her, not ever having a cold seemed the most wonderful. That also meant never having the flu, and—"You can't get AIDS!"

"That's right. We run hotter than humans, too. My temperature is usually at or above a hundred degrees. The weather has to get really, really cold before I get uncomfortable."

"That's so unfair," she complained. "I want to be immune to colds and AIDS, too."

"No measles," he murmured. "No chicken pox. No shingles. No cold sores." His eyes were dancing with merriment. "If you really want to be Raintree and never have a stuffy nose again, there's a way."

"How? Bury a chicken by the dark of the moon and run backward around a stump seven times?"

He paused, arrested by the image. "You have the strangest imagination."

"Tell me! How does someone become Raintree? What's the initiation ritual?"

"It's an old one. You've heard of it."

"The chicken one is the only one I know. C'mon, what is it?"

His smile was slow and heated. "Have my baby."

Chapter 21

Lorna went white, then red, then white again. "That isn't funny," she said in a stifled tone, getting up to prowl restlessly around the room. She picked up a pillow and fluffed it, but instead of placing it back on the sofa, she stood with it clasped to her chest, her head bowed over it.

"I'm not joking."

"You don't…you shouldn't have babies as a means to an end. People who don't want babies for themselves should never, never have them."

"Agreed," he said softly, leaving his spot by the windows and strolling toward her as unhurriedly as if he had no destination, no agenda.

"It's nothing to be taken lightly." That was a dirty game of pool he was playing, saying *Have my baby* as if he meant it. He couldn't mean it. They had known each other two days. That was something men said to seduce women, because hundreds of centuries ago some cunning bastard had figured out most women were pushovers for babies.

"I'm taking this very seriously, I promise." His tone was gentle as he touched her shoulder, curving his palm over the slope before sliding his hand over her back. She felt the heat transferring from his skin to hers, burning through her clothes. His fingertips sought out her spine, stroking downward, gently rubbing out the tension thrumming beneath her skin.

She hadn't known she was so tense, or that the gentle massage would turn her to butter. She let him urge her against him, let her head nestle into his shoulder, because everything about what he was doing felt so good. Still… She looked up at him with narrowed eyes. "Don't think I haven't noticed how close that hand's getting to my butt."

"I'd be disappointed if you hadn't." A smile curved his mouth as he pressed a warm kiss, then another, to her temple.

"Don't let it get any lower," she warned.

"Are you sure?" Beginning at the waistband of her jeans, he traced a finger down the center seam—down, down, pressing lightly, while his hot palm massaged her bottom. That finger left a trail of fire in its wake, made her squirm and shudder and begin, at least ten times, to say *No*. He would stop if she said it; the decision to continue or not was hers—but the security of knowing that was what kept the single word unsaid. Instead, all she did was gasp with agonized anticipation, and arch, and cling—waiting, waiting, focusing entirely on the slow progression of the caress, as his hand slowly slid down to dip between her legs from behind. He pressed harder then, his fingers rubbing against her entrance through her jeans, so that the friction of the seam lightly abraded flesh that was soft and yielding.

He had been bringing her to this point for two days, since that first kiss in his kitchen, patiently feeding the spark of desire until it became a small flame, then keeping the flame going with fleeting touches and something even harder to resist: his open desire for her. She could recognize what he was doing, see the subtle progressions, and even appreciate the mastery of his restraint. Getting into bed with her last night—and then not touching her—had been diabolically intelligent. Since the moment they'd met, he had forced her to do a lot of things, but not once had he tried to force her response. She would have shut him down cold if he had. The spark would have gone out, and she wouldn't have let it be resurrected.

His warm mouth moved along the line of her jaw, leisurely nipping and tasting, as if he wanted nothing more than this and had all the time in the world in which to savor her. Only the rock-hard bulge in his jeans betrayed any urgency, and she was pressed so tightly to him that she could feel every twitch, every throb, that invited her to part her legs and let him get even closer.

Then his mouth closed over hers and the last shred of restraint dissolved. The kiss was hard and deep and hungry, his tongue taking her mouth. Desire sizzled along her nerves, turned her warm and yielding and boneless. His free hand moved to her breasts, found her nipples through the layers of cloth, gently pinched them awake. He had her now; she wasn't restraining him from any caress, and the clothing that kept his body from hers was suddenly maddening. She wanted the rest of it, all he had to give her, and with a burst of clarity, she knew she had to say what she wanted to say *now*. A minute from now would be too late.

The proof of how far gone she was came in the amount of willpower it took for her to tear her mouth from his. "We need to talk," she said, her voice strained and husky.

He groaned and laughed at the same time. "Oh,

God," he muttered, frustration raw in his tone. "The four words guaranteed to strike fear in any man. Can't it wait?"

"No—it's about this. Us. Now."

He heaved a sigh and pressed his forehead against hers. "Your timing is sadistic, you know that?"

Lorna slid her hands into the black silk of his hair, feeling the coolness of the strands, the heat of his scalp. "Your fault. I almost forgot." Her tongue felt a little thick, her speech slower than normal. Yes, this was definitely his fault, all of it.

"Let's have it, then." Resignation lay heavy in the words, the resignation of a simple male who just wanted to have sex. She would have laughed, if not for the heavy pull of desire that threatened to overwhelm everything else.

She swallowed, struggled to get the words lined up in her head so she could say them coherently. "My answer…to whether or not we do this…depends on you."

"I vote yes," he replied, biting her earlobe.

"This mind-control thing…you have to stop. I can be your prisoner or your lover, but I won't be both."

He lifted his head then, his gaze going cool and sharp. "There's no compulsion involved in this. I'm not forcing you." Anger clipped his words.

"I know," she said, drawing a shuddering breath.

"I can tell the difference, believe me. It's… I have to have the choice, whether to stay or go. The freedom has to be there. You can't keep moving me around like a puppet."

"It was necessary."

"At first. I hated it then, I hate it now, but you did have valid reasons *at first*. You don't now. I think you're too used to having your way in everything, *Dranir*."

"You would have run," he said flatly.

"My choice." She couldn't bend on this. Dante Raintree was a force of nature; dealing with him in a relationship would be challenging enough even without his ability to chain her with a thought. He had to bow to her free will or their only relationship could be jailer and prisoner. "We're equals…or we're nothing."

Reading him wasn't easy, but she could see he didn't like relinquishing control at all. Intuitively, she grasped his dilemma. On a purely intellectual basis, he understood. On a more primitive level, he didn't want to lose her, and he was prepared to be as autocratic and heavy-handed as necessary.

"All or nothing." She met his gaze, squaring up with him like fighters in a boxing ring. "You can't use mind control on me *ever again*. I'm not your enemy. At some point you have to trust me, and that point is now. Or were you planning to keep me pinned forever?"

"Not forever." He ground out the words. "Just until—"

"Until what?"

"Until you wanted to stay."

She smiled at that rough admission and gripped both hands in his hair. "I want to stay," she said simply, and kissed his chin. "But at some point I may want to go. You have to take that chance, and if that day does come, you have to let me go. I'm taking the same chance with you, that one day you may not want me around. I want your word. Promise me you'll never use mind control on me again."

She saw his fury and frustration, saw his jaw work as he ground his teeth. She knew what she was asking of him; giving up a power went against every instinct he had, as both a man and a Dranir. He lived in two worlds, both the normal and the paranormal, and in both he was boss. As understated as he kept things, he was still boss. If he hadn't been the Raintree Dranir, his natural dominance would have been reined in more, but reality was what it was, and he was a king in that world.

Abruptly he dropped his arms from around her and stepped back. His eyes were narrowed and fierce. "You may go."

Lorna barely controlled a protest at the loss of his touch, his heat. What was he saying? "Are you giving me your permission—or an order?"

"A promise."

Breathing was abruptly difficult. Her lips trembled, and she firmed them, started to speak, but he lifted a hand to stop her. "One thing."

"What?"

The green of his eyes almost glowed, they were so intent. "If you stay...the brakes are off."

Fair warning, she thought dizzily, shivering a little in anticipation. "I'm staying," she managed to say, taking half a step forward.

A half step was all she had time to take before he moved, an explosion of pent-up power that was now released from all constraint. If she was free, then so was he. He swung her off her feet and carried her into the bedroom, moving so fast her head swam. The slow, careful seduction was over, and all that was left was raw desire. He tossed her on the bed and followed her down, pulling at her clothes, his movements rough with urgency, even though she helped him, her own hands shaking as she dealt with buttons and zippers, hooks and laces. He jerked her shoes and jeans off as she fought to unbutton his shirt, peeled her underwear down her legs while she struggled to lower his zipper, hampered by the thrust of his erection.

He shoved his jeans and boxers down, and kicked them away. Lorna tried to reach for him, tried to stroke him, but he was a tidal wave that flattened her on the bed and crushed her under his heavy weight. His penetration wasn't careful, it was hard and fast and powerful, taking him deep.

She gave a choked cry, her body shocked by the impact even as she rose to meet it. His heat burned her, inside and out. He pulled out, thrust in again, then again. Her brain stuttered a warning of what that heat meant, and she managed to say, "Condom."

He swore, pulled out, and jerked open a drawer in the bedside table. He tore the first condom, rolling it on. Swearing even more, he slowed down, took more care with the second one. When he was safely sheathed, he pushed into her again, then held her crushed to him, their bodies straining together as relief shuddered through them. Tears rolled down her face. This wasn't an orgasm, it was…pure relief, as if unrelenting pain had suddenly vanished. It was completion—not a sexual one, but something that went deeper, as if some part of her had been missing and suddenly was there.

It was being filled, when she hadn't realized how empty she was; fed, when she hadn't known she was hungry.

He rose, supporting his weight on his arms as he pulled back, then eased forward in a slow, deep

thrust. "Don't cry," he murmured, kissing the tears
from her wet face.

"I'm not," she said. "It's just leakage."

"Ah."

He said it as if he understood, and maybe he did.
He snagged her gaze and held it as he moved in and
out, drawing her response to him, going deep to
find more. She was both relaxed and tense at the
same time: relaxed because she knew he wasn't
going to leave her behind, and tense from the
building pleasure.

It happened faster than she'd thought possible.
Instead of hovering just out of reach, building
slowly, she came hard in a rush of sensation that
roared through her entire body. Dante slipped his
own leash, driving fast and deep, and followed.

When she was able to breathe again, able to
open her eyes, the first thing she saw was fire.
Every candle in the room was flaming.

"Tell me why you denied your gift."

They were lying entwined, her head on his
shoulder, barely recovered from what had felt so
cataclysmic that neither of them had spoken for a
long time. Instead they had been slowly stroking
each other, touch replacing words, touches of re-
assurance and comfort, of silent joy.

She sighed, for the first time in her life feeling

a little distance from the unhappiness of her childhood. "I think you already know. It's not an original story, or an interesting one."

"Probably not. Tell me anyway."

She smiled against his shoulder, glad he wasn't making any big deal of it, though the smile faded almost as fast as it had bloomed. Talking about her mother was difficult, even though it had been fifteen years since she'd last seen her. Maybe it would never be easy, but at least the pain and fear were less immediate.

"As bad as it was, a lot of kids have it worse. The only reason she didn't abort me was so she could get that monthly check. She told me that every month when it came. She'd shake the envelope at me and say, 'This is the only reason you're alive, you freak.' That check helped keep her in drugs and booze."

He didn't say anything, though his mouth tightened.

Her head found a more comfortable resting spot on his shoulder, and she nestled against him, soaking up his heat. She'd known he felt hot, but it was nice to know she hadn't been imagining things. "It was constant slaps, and she'd throw things at me—cups, empty wine bottles, a can opener. Whatever was near. Once she threw a can of chicken noodle soup, hit me in the head, and knocked me out. I had a headache for days. And she wouldn't let me have any of the soup."

"How old were you?"

"That time…six, I think. I'd started school and discovered numbers. Sometimes I was so excited I'd have to tell someone what I'd learned about the numbers that day, and she was the only someone I had. She told my teacher I'd fallen and hit my head on the curb."

"You'd have been better off in foster care," he growled.

"I ended up there when I was sixteen. She took off one day and never came back. I remember… even though she'd made it plain how much she hated me, when she left it was as if part of me was missing, because she was what I knew. By that time I wasn't helpless, but when I was little…no matter how bad it is, little kids will do anything to hold on to what passes for a family, you know?" She sighed. "I know I overreacted about the baby thing. I'm sorry. You said 'baby,' and that's one of my triggers."

A little smile curved his mouth. "Don't get upset again, but I wasn't joking. When a human mother gives birth to a Raintree baby, she becomes Raintree. No, I don't understand the science of it. Something to do with hormones and the mixing of blood, and the baby being a genetic dominant.

I'm not sure there *is* any science to explain it. Magic doesn't need to be logical."

The explanation intrigued her. Everything she'd learned about the Raintree intrigued her. It was such a different world, a different experience, and yet they existed normally within the regular world—not that the regular world knew about them, because if that ever came about, then their existence would not only not be normal but they might cease to exist at all. Lorna had few illusions about the world she lived in. "What about human men who have babies with Raintree women? What changes them?"

"Nothing," Dante said. "They stay human."

That didn't seem fair, and she said so. Dante shrugged. "Life isn't perfect. You deal with it."

Wasn't that the truth. She knew about dealing. She also knew that, right now, she was very happy.

The dozen or so candles in the room were putting out enough heat that she was beginning to be uncomfortable. Looking around at them, she realized that Dante and fire went hand in hand. She didn't like fire, would always be afraid of it, but…life wasn't perfect. You dealt with it.

"Can you put out those candles?" she asked.

He lifted his head from the pillow and looked at them, as if he hadn't realized they were burning.

"Damn. Yeah, no problem." Just like that, they went out, the wicks gently smoking.

Lorna climbed on top of him and kissed him, smiling as she felt a leap of interest against her inner thigh. "Now, big boy, let's see if you can light them again."

Chapter 22

Sunday morning

She had stayed.

Dante came back into the bedroom from the balcony where he'd met the sunrise, intense satisfaction filling him as he saw Lorna still peacefully asleep in his bed. Only the top half of her head was visible, dark red hair vivid against the white pillow, but he was acutely aware of what it meant for even that much to not be covered by the sheet.

She was feeling safer. Not completely safe, not yet, but safer. When he was in the bed with her, she slept stretched out, relaxed, cuddled against him. When he left the bed, though, within five minutes she was curled in a tight, protective ball. One day—maybe not this week or this month, or even this year, but one day—he hoped he could see her sprawled in sleep, head uncovered, maybe no covers at all. Then he would know she felt safe.

And when the day came that he didn't feel the need to constantly check on her whereabouts, he would know that he felt safe, too.

He *didn't* constantly check on her; his pride refused to let him do that to either her or himself, but the need, the anxiety, was always there.

On Wednesday she hadn't gone with him. He'd called the Jaguar dealership and had a new car sent over, and she had stayed there to accept it. The salesman had called his cell phone to let him know delivery had been made, but Dante had expected Lorna to also call and let him know. She hadn't. Since he had also had her own car—a dinged-up, slightly rusty red Corolla—delivered that morning, he'd been acutely aware that she was free, she had wheels, and she had cash in her pocket. If she wanted to leave, he couldn't stop her. He'd given his word.

He'd wanted to call, just to reassure himself that she was still there, but he hadn't. She could walk out as soon as the call ended, so talking to her at any given time was useless. The only thing he could do, *would* do, was hope. And pray.

He hadn't cut his work short. No matter what happened, whether she stayed or left, the work had to be done. Consequently, it was almost sunset when he drove up to see her car still parked in his garage, with his brand-new Jaguar sitting outside, exposed to the sun and blowing grit. As he'd zoomed the Lotus into its slot, all he'd been aware of was a relief so intense that he'd almost been weak with it. Let the Jaguar sit out; seeing her Corolla still there was worth more to him than any car, no matter how expensive.

She'd met him at the kitchen door, wearing a pair of cutoffs and one of his silk shirts, a scowl on her face. "It's eight-thirty. I'm starving. Do you work this late on a regular basis? Got any idea what we're going to do for dinner?"

He'd laughed and pounced, and showed her exactly what he wanted to eat for dinner. She hadn't said another word about food until after ten.

On Thursday, she'd gone to the hotel with him. Work was continuing at a frantic pace. He'd gotten the okay to bulldoze the charred ruins of the casino so he could begin rebuilding, and things were so hectic he'd actually delegated some authority to her, because he couldn't be in two places at once. On a perverse level, he'd enjoyed watching her give orders to Al Franklin. Al, being Al, was sanguine about everything, but Lorna got a great deal of satisfaction from the arrangement, and he'd got a great deal of enjoyment from her satisfaction.

At lunch, they'd gone to his suite and lit candles. Twice.

On Friday, she didn't go with him, and he'd sweated through that day, too. When he got home, his relief at seeing her car still there had been as acute as it had been on Wednesday, and that was when he faced the truth.

He loved her. This wasn't just sex, just a brief affair, or *just* anything. It was the real deal. He loved her courage, her gallantry, her grumpiness. He loved the snarky comments, the stubbornness and the vulnerability she hated for anyone to see.

Gideon would laugh his ass off when he found out, not just because Dante had fallen so far, but out of sheer relief that at long last, and if the angels smiled, he might soon lose his position as heir apparent.

The bottom dropped out of Dante's stomach and his gut clenched. Last night he'd been rolling on a condom when abruptly he knew that he didn't want to wear protection. Lorna had been watching him, waiting, and she'd noticed his long hesitation. Finally, without a word, he'd pulled off the condom and tossed it aside, then steadily met her gaze. If she wanted him to put on another one, he would; the choice was hers.

She had reached out and pulled him down and

into her. Just remembering the intense half hour that had followed turned him on so much that the candle beside the bed flared to life.

Today was the solstice, and he felt as if he could set the world on fire, as if his skin would burst from all the power boiling inside him. He wanted to pull her under him and ride her until he was completely empty, until she had taken everything he had to give. First, though, they had to have a very serious talk. Last night they'd done something that was too important for them to let drift along.

As he sat down on the edge of the bed, he extinguished the candle, because a candle that was already lit was useless as a barometer of his control. This conversation might be emotionally charged, so he would have to be very careful.

He slid his hand under the sheet and touched her bare thigh. "Lorna. Wake up."

He felt her tense, as always; then she relaxed, and one sleepy hazel eye blinked open and glared at him over the edge of the sheet. "Why? It's Sunday, the day of rest. I'm resting. Go away."

He tugged the sheet down. "Wake up. Breakfast is ready."

"It is not. You're lying. You've been on the balcony." She grabbed the sheet and pulled it over her head.

"How do you know that, if you've been asleep?"

"I didn't say I was sleeping, I said I was resting."

"Eating isn't considered work. Come on. I have fresh orange juice, coffee, the bagels are already toasted, and the sunrise is great."

"To *you*, maybe, but it's *five-thirty* on Sunday morning, and I don't want to eat breakfast this early. I want one day a week when you don't drag me out of bed at the crack of dark-thirty."

"Next Sunday you can sleep, I promise." Rather than fight her for custody of the sheet, he slid his hand under the covers, found her thigh again and swiftly reached upward to pinch her ass.

She squeaked and bolted out of bed, rubbing her backside. "Payback will be hell," she warned, as she pushed her disheveled hair out of her face and stalked off to the bathroom.

He imagined it would be. Dante grinned as he returned to the balcony.

She came out five minutes later, wrapped in his thick robe and still scowling. She wasn't wearing anything under the robe, so he enjoyed glimpses as she plopped into a chair across from him. It also gaped at the neck, revealing the gold chain from which hung the protection charm he'd given her on Wednesday night. He'd made it specifically for her, out here on the balcony, and let her watch. She'd been enthralled at the way he cupped the charm and held it up so his breath warmed it as he murmured a few words in Gaelic. The charm had taken on a gentle green glow that quickly faded. When he slipped the chain over her head she had fingered the charm, looking as if she might cry. She hadn't taken it off since.

As grumpy as she was when she first woke, she didn't stay that way for long. By the time she'd had her second bite of bagel she was looking much more cheerful. Still, he waited until she'd finished the bagel and her juice glass was empty before he said, "Will you marry me?"

She had much the same reaction as when he'd mentioned a baby. She paled, then turned red, then jumped out of her chair and went to stand at the railing with her back to him. Dante knew a lot about women, but more specifically, he knew Lorna, so he didn't leave her standing there alone. He caged her with his arms, putting his hands on top of hers on the railing, not holding her tightly but giving her his warmth. "Is the question that hard to answer?"

He felt her shoulders heave. Alarmed, he turned her around. Tears were streaking down her face. "Lorna?"

She wasn't sobbing, but her lips were trembling. "I'm sorry," she said, swiping at her face. "I know this is silly. It's just—no one has ever wanted me before."

"I doubt that. Probably you just didn't notice them wanting you. I wanted you the minute I saw you."

"Not that kind of wanting." Another tear leaked down. "The other kind, the staying-around kind."

"I love you," he said gently, mentally cursing the bitch who had given birth to her for not nurturing the sense of security that every child should have, the knowledge that, no matter what, someone loved her and wanted her.

"I know. I believe you." She gulped. "I sort of figured it out when you deliberately wrecked your Jaguar to protect me."

"I knew I could buy another car," he said simply.

"That's when I knew that you'd ruined me, that I wouldn't be able to leave unless you threw me out. I kept hoping it was just old-fashioned lust I was feeling, but I knew better, and it scared me to death." She gave a shaky laugh, despite the slow roll of yet another tear. "In just two days, you'd ruined me."

He rubbed the side of his nose. "We hadn't had much time together, but it was quality time."

"Quality!" She gaped at him, mouth open. Indignation dried her tears. "You manhandled me, dragged me into a fire, tore open my head and smashed my brain flat, tore off my clothes and kept me a prisoner!"

"I didn't say it was good quality. You have a

way with words, you know that? 'Tore open your head,' my ass."

"You don't like it when I call it 'brain-rape,'" she said sourly. "And I think I have a better grasp of how it felt than you do."

"I guess you do, at that. When you voluntarily link with someone, it doesn't—"

"Good God." She looked horrified. "Some of you actually do that *willingly?*"

"I told you, it doesn't hurt when it's done right. If someone needs to boost their power, they find someone else who is willing to link. Every so often Gideon and I go home to Sanctuary, and we link with Mercy to perform a protection spell over the homeplace. Doing it right takes time, but it doesn't hurt. Will you answer the—"

"I hope you have some kind of law against doing it without permission."

"Uh—no."

She looked horrified. "You mean you Raintree people can just go around breaking into people's heads, and nobody does anything about it?"

He was beginning to feel frustrated. Would the woman never answer his question? "I didn't say that. Very few of us are strong enough to over-power someone else's brain unless they cooperate."

"And you're one of those few," she said sarcastically. "Right. Lucky me."

"Specifically, only the royal family. Which I've asked you to join, I'd like to point out, if you'll answer the damn question!"

She smiled, and it was like a ray of sunshine breaking across her lively, mobile face. "Of course I will. Did you really doubt it?"

"I never know which way you'll jump. I thought you might love me, because you stayed. Then, last night—" He flicked a finger over her chin. "Not telling me to wear a condom was a dead giveaway."

She stared at him, a peculiar expression stealing over her face.

He straightened, instantly alert. "What's wrong?" Just that quickly she looked sick, as if she were going to throw up.

She rubbed her arms, frowning. "I'm cold. It's that same—" She broke off, her eyes widening with horror, and before he could react she threw herself bodily at him, catching him unprepared for the impact of her weight. He caught her, staggering back, then lurching to the side as he tried to catch his balance and failed. They fell to the floor of the balcony in a tangle of arms, legs and bathrobe as the French door behind him shattered. Hard on the explosion of glass came a sharp, flat retort that echoed through the mountains.

Rifle fire.

Dante wrapped his arms around Lorna, got his feet under him and lunged through the shattered door just as another shot spatted into the side of the house where they had been. Then he rolled with her, getting her away from the wall, before finally lunging to his feet and dragging her out into the hall. "Stay down!" he yelled at her when she tried to stand, pushing her flat again.

His mind was racing. The fire. The gang shooting when he and Lorna so conveniently happened to be boxed in the kill zone. Now someone was shooting at him again. These weren't a series of accidents; they were all related. The fire marshal hadn't found any evidence of arson, which meant—

A Fire-Master didn't need accelerants to start a fire, or to keep it going. Someone, or several someones, had been feeding the fire; that was why he hadn't been able to extinguish it. If he hadn't used mind control for the first time just minutes before trying to control the fire and hadn't known how it would affect him, if he hadn't suspected Lorna might be Ansara, he would have figured it out right away.

Ansara! He snarled his rage. It had to be them. Several of them must have gotten together and decided to try burning him out. They'd known he would engage the fire, that he wouldn't give up until it overwhelmed him. If Lorna hadn't been there, the plan would have worked, too, but they hadn't counted on her.

The cold, sick feeling she kept getting—that was when any Ansara were nearby.

"There was a red dot on your forehead," she said, though her teeth were chattering so hard she could barely speak, or maybe that was because he was practically kneeling on her back to keep her down.

A laser targeting system, then. This wasn't simply seizing an opportunity, but actively planning and pursuing.

The sniper had failed. What would they try next? He had to assume there was more than one Ansara out there, had to assume there was a backup plan. They wouldn't try to burn him out again, since the first effort had failed; they would think he had sufficient power to handle any flame they could muster. But what *would* they do?

Whatever it was, he couldn't let them succeed, not with Lorna here.

"Stay here," he commanded, getting to his feet.

She scrambled after him. The woman didn't obey worth a damn. "I said stay here!" he roared, whirling back and catching her arm, pushing her down once more. He started to stick her ass to the floor with a mental command, but he'd promised her—damn it, he'd *promised* her—and he couldn't do it.

"I was going to call the cops!" she shouted at

him, so furious at his rough handling that she was practically levitating.

"Don't bother. This isn't something the cops can handle. Stay here, Lorna. I don't want you caught between us."

"Who is *us?*" she yelled at his back as he charged down the stairs. "What are you going to do?"

"Fight fire with fire," he said grimly.

Dante had a tremendous advantage. This was his home, his property, and he knew every inch of it. Because he was Raintree, because he was the Dranir and took precautions, he went out through the tunnel he'd built under his house. He knew where he'd been standing when the laser scope had settled the telltale dot on his forehead, so he had a good idea where the shooter had been standing, too.

There was only one. He hadn't found signs of any others.

He had no intention of trying to capture the bastard or engaging him in any sort of face-to-face battle. He prowled up the ravine like a big cat, death in his eyes. The shooter's position must have been just around this cut, maybe in that big cluster of rocks. A sniper needed a stable shooting platform, and those rocks would be convenient. This ravine provided good cover, too, for approaching.

And for leaving.

Dante slid around the cut and came face-to-face with a man wearing desert camo and toting a rifle. He didn't hesitate at all. The man had barely moved, bringing the rifle up to fire, when Dante set him aflame.

The screams were raw and terrified. The man dropped the rifle and threw himself to the ground, frantically rolling, but Dante ruthlessly kept the fire going. This bastard had come close to killing Lorna, and there was no mercy in his heart for anyone who harmed her. In seconds the screams became howls, taking on an inhuman quality—and then silence.

Dante extinguished the flame.

The man lay smoldering, barely recognizable as human.

Dante used his foot to roll the man onto his back. Incredibly, hate-filled eyes glared up at him from the charred face. The hole that had been the man's mouth worked, and a ghostly sound tore from a throat that shouldn't have worked.

"Toooo late. Toooo late."

Then he died, massive shock stopping his heart. Dante stood frozen, his thoughts working furiously.

Too late? Too late for what?

He'd touched the Ansara. The man had been in

agony, his hate projected like a force field, and Dante had read him.

Too late.

He could warn Mercy, but it would be too late.

"Oh, shit," he said softly, and ran.

Lorna had obeyed him, and stayed put. She was in the kitchen, crouched by the refrigerator, when he charged in and grabbed the nearest phone. His first phone call was to Mercy. His second was to Gideon, who could get to Mercy much faster than he could.

Because it was the solstice, because Gideon's personal electrical field played hell with all electronics, when Gideon answered the phone almost all Dante could hear was static.

"Get to Mercy!" he roared, hoping Gideon would understand anyway. "The Ansara are attacking Sanctuary!" Then he slammed down the phone and tore open the door to the garage, his mind racing.

The corporate jet would get him to the airport nearest Sanctuary in about four hours. He could try Gideon again from the plane.

Two hundred years ago the Ansara had tried to destroy the Raintree and had failed. Now they were trying again, and, damn it, this time they might succeed in destroying Sanctuary—where Mercy was, with Eve.

"Where are you going?" Lorna shrieked as he got in the Lotus.

"Stay here!" he ordered one last time, and reversed out of the garage. He didn't want Lorna anywhere near Sanctuary. He didn't know if he would make it back alive, but no matter what, he had to know she was safe.

"I don't think so," Lorna muttered furiously as she changed clothes. Dante Raintree wasn't the only person who knew how to get things done. If he thought he could leave her behind while he went to fight some sort of supernatural battle, well, he would soon find out he was wrong.

* * * * *

Turn the page for a special preview
of the final two titles in the Raintree Trilogy,
RAINTREE: HAUNTED
by national bestselling author
Linda Winstead Jones and
RAINTREE: SANCTUARY
by New York Times bestselling author
Beverly Barton

Look for
RAINTREE: HAUNTED
in June 2007 and
RAINTREE: SANCTUARY
in July 2007
only from Silhouette Nocturne

Monday Morning, 3:37 a.m.

When Gideon's phone rang in the middle of the night, it meant someone was dead. "Raintree," he answered, his voice rumbling with the edges of sleep.

"Sorry to wake you."

Surprised to hear his brother Dante's voice, Gideon came instantly awake. "What's wrong?"

"There's a fire at the casino. Could be worse," Dante added before Gideon could ask, "but it's bad enough. I didn't want you to see it on the morning news without some warning. Call Mercy in a couple of hours and tell her I'm all right. I'd call her myself, but I'm going to have my hands full for the next few days."

Gideon sat up, wide awake. "If you need me, I'm there."

"No, thanks. You've got no business getting on an airplane this week, and everything here is fine. I just wanted to call you before I got so tied up in red tape I couldn't get to a phone."

Gideon ran his fingers through his hair. Outside his window, the waves of the Atlantic crashed and rolled. He offered again to go to Reno and help. He could drive, if necessary. But once again Dante told him everything was fine, and they ended the call. Gideon reset his alarm for five-thirty. He would call Mercy before she started her day. The fire must have been a bad one for Dante to be so certain it would make the national news.

Alarm reset, Gideon fell back onto the bed. Maybe he'd sleep, maybe not. He listened to the ocean waves and let his mind wander. With the solstice coming in less than a week, his normal electric abnormalities were really out of whack. The surges usually spiraled out of control only when a ghost was nearby, but for the past few days—and for the week to come—it didn't take the addition of an electrically charged spirit to make appliances and electronics—or planes—in his path go haywire. There was nothing he could do but be cautious. Maybe he should take a few days off, stay away from the station altogether and lie low. He closed his eyes and fell back asleep.

She appeared without warning, floating over the end of the bed and smiling down at him, as she always did. Tonight she wore a plain white dress that touched her bare ankles, and her long dark hair was unbound. Emma, as she said she would one day be called, always came to him in the form of a child. She was very much unlike the ghosts who haunted him. This child came only in dreams and was untainted by the pain of life's hardships. She carried with her no need for justice, no heartbreak, no gnawing deed left undone. Instead, she brought with her light and love, and a sense of peace. And she insisted on calling him Daddy.

"Good morning, Daddy."

Gideon sighed and sat up. He'd first seen this particular spirit three months ago, but lately her visits had become more and more frequent. More and more real. Who knew. Maybe he had been her father in another life, but he wasn't going to be anyone's daddy in this one.

"Good morning, Emma."

The spirit of the little girl drifted down to stand on the foot of the bed. "I'm so excited." She laughed, and the sound was oddly familiar. Gideon liked that laugh. It made his heart do strange things. He convinced himself that the sense of warm familiarity meant nothing. Nothing at all.

"Why are you excited?"

"I'm coming to you soon, Daddy."

He closed his eyes and sighed. "Emma, honey, I've told you a hundred times, I'm not going to have kids in this lifetime, so you can stop calling me Daddy."

She just laughed again. "Don't be silly, Daddy. You always have me."

The spirit who had told him that her name would be Emma in this lifetime did have the Raintree eyes, his own dark brown hair and a touch of honey in her skin. But he knew better than to trust what he saw. After all, she only showed up in dreams. He was going to have to stop eating nachos before going to bed.

"I hate to tell you this, sweetheart, but in order to make a baby there has to be a mommy as well as a daddy. I'm not getting married and I'm not having kids, so you'll just have to choose someone else to be your daddy this time around."

Emma was not at all perturbed. "You're always so stubborn. I am coming to you, Daddy, I am. I'm coming to you in a moonbeam."

Gideon had tried romantic relationships before, and they never worked. He had to hide so much of himself from the women in his life; it would never do to have someone that close. And a family? Forget it. He already had to answer to the new chief, the rest of his family and a never-ending stream of ghosts. He wasn't about to put himself in a position where he would be obligated to answer to anyone else. Women came and went, but he made sure none ever got too close or stayed too long.

It was Dante's job to reproduce, not his. Gideon glanced toward the dresser, where the latest fertility charm sat ready to be packaged up and mailed. Once Dante had kids of his own, Gideon would no longer be next in line for the position of Dranir, head of the Raintree family. He couldn't think of anything worse than being Dranir, except maybe getting married and having kids of his own.

Big brother had his hands full at the moment, though, so maybe he would hold off a few days before mailing that charm. Maybe.

"Be careful," Emma said as she floated a bit closer. "She's very bad, Daddy. Very bad. You have to be careful."

"Don't call me Daddy," Gideon said. As an afterthought he added, "Who's very bad?"

"You'll know soon. Take care of my moonbeam, Daddy."

"On a moonbeam," he said softly. "What a load of…"

"It's just begun," Emma said, her voice and her body fading away.

* * * * *

Turn the page
for your first look at
RAINTREE: SANCTUARY
by New York Times *bestselling author*
Beverly Barton

Mercy Raintree sat on the firm, grassy ground, her eyes closed, her hands resting in her lap. Whenever she was troubled, she came to Amadahy Pointe to meditate, to collect her thoughts and renew her strength. The sunshine covered her like an invisible robe, wrapping her in light and warmth. The spring breeze caressed her tenderly, like a lover's soft touch. With her eyes closed and her soul open to the positive energy she drew from this holy place, this sanctuary within a sanctuary, she focused on what was most important to her.

Family.

Mercy sensed impending danger. But from

whom or from what, she did not know. Although her greatest talents lay in being an empath and a healer, she possessed latent precognitive powers, less erratic than her cousin Echo's, but not as strong. She had also been cursed with the ability to sense the emotional and physical condition of others from a distance. *Clairempathy.* As a child, she'd found her various empathic talents maddening, but gradually, year by year, she had learned to control them. And now, despite both Dante and Gideon blocking her from intercepting their thoughts and emotions, she could still manage to pick up something on the outer fringes of each brother's individual consciousness.

Dante and Gideon were in trouble. But she did not know why. Perhaps it was nothing more than stress from their chosen professions. Or it could even be problems in their personal lives.

If her brothers thought she could help them, they would ask her to intervene. That knowledge reassured her that their problems were within the realm of human reality and not of a supernatural nature. Her brothers were, as they had pointed out to her on numerous occasions, grown men, perfectly capable of taking care of themselves without the assistance of their baby sister.

Past experience had taught her that when their souls needed replenishing, their spirits nurtured, her brothers came home, here to the Raintree land, deep in the North Carolina mountains. The homeplace was protected by a powerful magic that had been established by their ancestors two centuries ago after The Battle. Within the boundaries of these secure acres, no living creature could intrude without alerting the resident guardian. Mercy Raintree was that guardian, protector of the homeplace, as her great-aunt Gillian had been until her death at a hundred and nineteen, and like Gillian's mother, Vesta, the first keeper of the Sanctuary in the early eighteen hundreds.

Taking a deep, cleansing breath, Mercy opened her eyes and looked at the valley below, spread out before her like a banquet feast. Late springtime in the mountains. An endless blue sky that went on forever. Towering green trees, the ancient, the old and the young growing together, reaching heavenward. Verdant life, thick and rich and sweet to the senses. A multitude of wildflowers blooming in abundance, their perfume tantalizing, their colors pleasing to the eye.

Mercy wasn't sure exactly what was wrong with her, but she felt a nagging sense of unease that had nothing to do with her brothers or with anyone in the Raintree tribe. No, the restlessness was within her, a yearning she was forced to control because of who she was, because of her duty to her family and to her people. Whenever these strange emotions unsettled her, she climbed the mountain to this sacred peak and meditated until the uncertainty subsided. But today, for some unknown reason, the anxiety clung to her.

Was it a warning?

Seven years ago, she had allowed that hunger inside her to lead her into dangerous territory, into a world she had been ill prepared for, into a relationship that had altered her life. She would not—could not—succumb to fear. And except for brief visits to Dante and Gideon, she would not leave the safety of the Raintree Sanctuary. Not ever again.

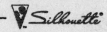

SPECIAL EDITION™

COMING IN JUNE

HER LAST FIRST DATE

by *USA TODAY* bestsellling author
SUSAN MALLERY

After one too many bad dates, Crissy Phillips
finally swore off men. Recently widowed,
pediatrician Josh Daniels can't risk losing his
heart. With an intense attraction pulling them
together, will their fear keep them apart?
Or will one wild night change everything...?

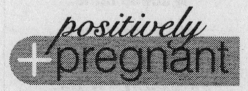

**Sometimes the unexpected
is the best news of all....**

Silhouette®

Romantic
SUSPENSE

**Sparked by Danger,
Fueled by Passion.**

*This month and every month look for
four new heart-racing romances
set against a backdrop of suspense!*

Romantic
SUSPENSE

**Sparked by Danger,
Fueled by Passion.**

Mission: Impassioned

A brand-new miniseries begins with

My Spy

By *USA TODAY* bestselling author

Marie Ferrarella

She had to trust him with her life....
It was the most daring mission of Joshua Lazlo's
career: rescuing the prime minister of England's
daughter from a gang of cold-blooded kidnappers.
But nothing prepared the shadowy secret agent
for a fiery woman whose touch ignited something
far more dangerous.

My Spy
#1472

Available July 2007 wherever you buy books!

HARLEQUIN®
Super Romance®

Acclaimed author
Brenda Novak
returns to Dundee, Idaho, with

COULDA BEEN A COWBOY

After gaining custody of his infant son,
professional athlete Tyson Garnier hopes to escape
the media and find some privacy in Dundee, Idaho.
He also finds Dakota Brown. But is she ready for the
potential drama that comes with him?

Also watch for:

BLAME IT ON THE DOG by Amy Frazier
(Singles...with Kids)

HIS PERFECT WOMAN by Kay Stockham

DAD FOR LIFE by Helen Brenna
(A Little Secret)

MR. IRRESISTIBLE by Karina Bliss

WANTED MAN by Ellen K. Hartman

Available June 2007 wherever Harlequin books are sold!

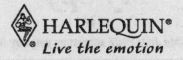

HARLEQUIN®
Live the emotion

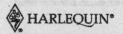

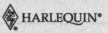
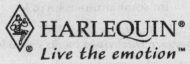

REQUEST YOUR FREE BOOKS!

2 FREE NOVELS PLUS 2 FREE GIFTS!

Silhouette®

n o c t u r n e™

Dramatic and Sensual Tales of Paranormal Romance.

YES! Please send me 2 FREE Silhouette® Nocturne™ novels and my 2 FREE gifts. After receiving them, if I don't wish to receive any more books, I can return the shipping statement marked "cancel." If I don't cancel, I will receive 4 brand-new novels every other month and be billed just $4.47 per book in the U.S. or $4.99 per book in Canada, plus 25¢ shipping and handling per book plus applicable taxes, if any*. That's a savings of about 15% off the cover price! I understand that accepting the 2 free books and gifts places me under no obligation to buy anything. I can always return a shipment and cancel at any time. Even if I never buy another book from Silhouette, the two free books and gifts are mine to keep forever.

238 SDN ELS4 338 SDN ELXG

Name _____ (PLEASE PRINT)

Address _____ Apt. #

City _____ State/Prov. _____ Zip/Postal Code

Signature (if under 18, a parent or guardian must sign)

Mail to the **Silhouette Reader Service™**:
IN U.S.A.: P.O. Box 1867, Buffalo, NY 14240-1867
IN CANADA: P.O. Box 609, Fort Erie, Ontario L2A 5X3

Not valid to current Silhouette Nocturne subscribers.

Want to try two free books from another line?
Call 1-800-873-8635 or visit www.morefreebooks.com.

* Terms and prices subject to change without notice. NY residents add applicable sales tax. Canadian residents will be charged applicable provincial taxes and GST. This offer is limited to one order per household. All orders subject to approval. Credit or debit balances in a customer's account(s) may be offset by any other outstanding balance owed by or to the customer. Please allow 4 to 6 weeks for delivery.

Your Privacy: Silhouette is committed to protecting your privacy. Our Privacy Policy is available online at www.eHarlequin.com or upon request from the Reader Service. From time to time we make our lists of customers available to reputable firms who may have a product or service of interest to you. If you would prefer we not share your name and address, please check here. ☐

SN07

Silhouette

nocturne™

COMING NEXT MONTH

#17 RAINTREE: HAUNTED • Linda Winstead Jones
The Raintree Trilogy (Book 2 of 3)

Born with the ability to speak to earthbound spirits, Gideon Raintree made a startlingly good homicide detective. But when his newly assigned partner, Hope Malory, arrived in Wilmington, she saw Gideon as a mystery waiting to be unraveled—and was given her chance when the Ansara wizards came to hunt the forgotten son of the Raintree clan.

#18 UNBOUND • Lori Devoti

Risk Leidolf was a hellhound—a legendary creature who could take either human or canine form—and he was in bondage to a malevolent witch. But when the evil witch asked him to hunt down innocent Kara Shane and destroy her, the man within him rebelled. Risk quickly devised a plan that with success would break him free—but if it failed, he'd lose his humanity and the only woman he could ever love.

SNCNM0507